THEY'LL HANG BILLY
FOR SURE

Billy Reese, the West's most notorious desperado, was to stand trial in New Chance, high in the Rockies. From all compass-points came the curious and the greedy, the riff-raff of the frontier, and newspapermen from as far away as New York, Chicago, San Francisco. Suddenly, the marshal had two murders on his hands; a crazed killer was on the loose. But the Texas Trouble-Shooters were there, girding their loins for action.

MARSHALL GROVER

◆

THEY'LL HANG BILLY FOR SURE

A Larry & Stretch Western

Complete and Unabridged

LINFORD
Leicester

First published in Hong Kong in 1975 by
Horwitz Publications
Australia

First Linford Edition
published 1997
by arrangement with
Horwitz Publications Pty Limited
Australia

British Library CIP Data

Grover, Marshall
    Larry & Stretch: they'll hang Billy for sure.
    —Large print ed.—
    Linford western library
    1. Australian fiction—20th century
    2. Large type books
    I. Title
    823 [F]

    ISBN 0–7089–7987–4

Published by
F. A. Thorpe (Publishing) Ltd.
Anstey, Leicestershire

Set by Words & Graphics Ltd.
Anstey, Leicestershire
Printed and bound in Great Britain by
T. J. Press (Padstow) Ltd., Padstow, Cornwall

This book is printed on acid-free paper

1

The Appleyard Death Wish

FIFTEEN minutes from this moment, Larry Valentine would be saving a life. The tall Texans, veteran drifters both, ambled from the lobby to the front porch of the New Chance Hotel and contentedly surveyed the main street. It was 10.15 of a warm and sunny morning and Messrs Lawrence Valentine and Woodville Eustace Emerson, better known as Larry and Stretch, were at peace with the world. At least temporarily.

"New Chance," remarked the lean and gangling Stretch; he towered over his partner by a full 3 inches, which made Larry 6 feet 3. "Good name for a town, runt. Maybe a good sign, huh? A new chance for you and me?"

"We've said that before," Larry reminded him. "Remember Beecher's Ford and Duff's Dip? And Sweeney?"

"And all the other two-bit towns." Stretch nodded wistfully. "Why, sure. We could name many a quiet town, so quiet we could've settled and quit driftin'. Only, after we'd been there a while, them towns got to be plumb lively, no place for a couple peace-lovin' hombres like us. But maybe, here in New Chance, we'll get lucky."

"Maybe," shrugged Larry. "But don't count on it."

They built cigarettes and traded friendly nods with passersby, the dark-haired and brawny Larry and the stringy, un-including commonly tall Stretch, two nomads with a hankering for peace and quiet, but destined to find strife, danger and violence no matter where they roamed. Since the end of the Civil War, they had been 'on the drift', working when their bankroll was thin, and usually involved in the activity at which they were most

2

proficient — trouble-shooting, pitting their wits, fists and gun-skill against the scum of the outlaw trails. Law-breakers, every variety thereof, were their natural enemies; they had fought and defeated more desperadoes in the past 18 months than the average frontier lawman was apt to encounter in 5 years.

Somehow, they had endured the years of tension and hardship, developing an instinct for survival, an ability to get along with the ordinary folk of the frontier and, more importantly, a fatalistic sense of humor. And, always, they nursed this futile ambition, clinging to a vague hope of eventually defeating their hex, shaking off the urge to wander and at last taking root. Well, it was something to think about.

"Two days we've been here," drawled Stretch, as they lit their cigarettes. "It's a sizeable town, but it ain't exactly overcrowded, and that's why it's so peaceable."

"Must've been a boomer two, three years back," mused Larry. Eleven

3

minutes before his next confrontation with the Grim Reaper, he propped a shoulder against a porch-post and raised his eyes to the abandoned diggings, the shaftheads pock-marking the northern slope of New Chance Pass. "Jake claims it was too damn dangerous for any peace-lovin' citizen, miners raisin' hell every night of the week, only three lawmen against a couple hundred sharpers and tinhorns and hard cases. Honky tonks, five big hotels, near three dozen hell-houses. And the undertaker workin' overtime."

"It's still a sizeable town," said Stretch. "But now there's only one saloon and this one hotel, and the only undertaker is the feller that manages the stage depot — workin' part-time."

"Even so, that one saloon sells good booze," said Larry, shifting his gaze to the double-storied Eureka half-way along the next block east. "And, come to think of it . . . "

"Yeah." Stretch nodded cheerfully. "Not too early in the day for a couple

4

tall beers. And ain't Jake Sharney the friendliest barkeep we ever knew?"

Larry's handsome visage creased in a wry grin. It was 10.21 now and he felt fine. Sometimes his sixth sense failed him. He had no premonition of impending violence when he descended from the porch with his partner and sauntered across the street.

"Jake's like every other barkeep," was his drawled rejoinder. "We never met a barkeep we didn't like."

"Maybe so, but Jake's special," insisted Stretch.

On this point, Larry had to agree. Jake Sharney was no veteran barkeep. He had been tending bar only four years and might never have turned to that trade but for his lameness.

"Yeah, Jake's special."

"Used to tote a badge," mused Stretch. "Think of that."

Sparing only a casual glance for the weary-looking roan tied to the saloon hitch-rail, they nudged the batwing doors open and entered the barroom.

Perched on his high stool behind the bar, Jake accorded them a welcoming grin. He was running to fat, but still muscular, alert-eyed in middle age, his thatch still thick, if a mite grey at the temples.

The stranger was at the end of the bar, moodily studying his reflection in the mirror above the shelves, a lean, passably handsome jasper aged 30 or thereabouts, rigged in dust-smeared range clothes and working on a sizeable shot of rye. Cyrus Hindmarsh, the town marshal, shared a table near the entrance with Oley Craydon, a forlorn, taciturn citizen who kept the stage depot in operation and performed the duties of undertaker when needs be. Jake's boss, Roscoe Lippert, was conspicuous by his absence. The scrawny marshal and the depot-manager mumbled greetings without raising their eyes from their checker board.

"Mornin', Valentine — Emerson," mumbled Cyrus. "Your move, Oley."

6

"Don't hustle me," grunted Oley.

"Hustle you say." Cyrus shook his head sadly. "Ain't nobody hustlin' in New Chance since the mines and the stamp mill closed up."

The Texans propped elbows on the bar and watched Jake Sharney perform. Without asking, he was drawing beer into tall tankards.

"Whiskey before noon ain't a wise idea," he said brusquely. "Not even for a couple hellers like you."

A lawman-turned-barkeep. Yes, Jake was special in the eyes of the case-hardened drifters. Serving a hitch as deputy of a Utah township some 4 years ago, he had tangled with the infamous Reese gang of bank bandits and stage robbers, who left him sprawled in the dust with two .45 slugs in his right leg. The leg had been saved, but Jake was incapable of fast movement nowadays. Unable to sit a saddle, he had turned in his badge, traveled south into the New Mexico Rockies and found his niche in the boom town in high-walled New Chance Pass.

"I'll be a barkeep for the rest of my days, and I ain't complainin'," he remarked, watching them drink. "There's worse ways a man can earn a livin'."

At exactly 10.26, Larry finished his beer, ordered refills and asked,

"You ever miss the old days, Jake? I hear tell New Chance was mighty wild when you first arrived. But now it's gettin' to be a ghost town."

"Too quiet for you, Jake?" prodded Stretch.

"The hell with the old days." Jake grinned amiably. "Listen, we three wouldn't have been swappin' friendly talk, havin' a few laughs together, if you'd hit Calvintown while I was deputy-sheriff. We'd have been what they call natural enemies — a hard-nosed lawman lockin' horns with the Texas Trouble-Shooters. I've heard all about your big reputation and how you always raised hell with lawmen,

8

but I can afford to forget all that now, see?"

"Stretch, you're lookin' at a happy man," said Larry.

"Damm right," nodded Jake. "That's me. A happy man. Totin' a badge, you're bound to make enemies. Tendin' bar, you're every man's buddy. And that's how I like it."

"Think New Chance'll ever start growin' again, Jake?" asked Larry, as Jake drew their refills.

"I'll tell you," confided the barkeep. "If this town's gonna grow again, it better start damn soon. Population's down to under a hundred, and more citizens quittin' every week. Few more months and there'll only be a handful of us. Western Union office'll likely close up. The telegrapher, Jerry Webb, he's raisin' vegetables back of the office just to pass the time. No more business here. A stagecoach passin' through twice a week ain't enough to keep New Chance alive."

"So the mayor and his pals got

plenty to fret about," opined Stretch.

"They're frettin' about it right now," confided Jake. "Havin' a special emergency meetin' up at the Gazette office — Shell and Tweedy, Roscoe and Doc. But what can they do? Talkin' ain't gonna change anything."

It was 10.30 now.

Abruptly, the stranger at the end of the bar nudged his empty glass aside and said, loud enough for all to hear,

"Damn her beautiful hide — I'll finish it once and for all!"

He spoke so bitterly and with such grim determination that the warning signals clamored in Larry's brain. He was springing to action even as the stranger began emptying his holster, his sixth sense working overtime now. The man was cocking the Colt, raising it to his temple. Stretch, Jake, the marshal and Oley Craydon were temporarily frozen with shock, when Larry bounded along the short space separating him from the would-be suicide and grappled with him. He got his left hand to the raised Colt and wedged part of his thumb in front of the hammer just as the stranger's trigger-finger began contracting. His right flashed up, the palm jamming under the man's chin, forcing his head back.

The struggle was brief. Larry hooked a leg behind the man's knees and threw all his weight against him so that they crashed to the floor. Stretch, recovering from his shock, moved toward them, followed by the confused Marshal Hindmarsh. But Larry wasn't in need of help. By the time they reached him, he was pinning the stranger down, straddling his chest and in possession of the six-shooter. He eased the hammer down and offered the weapon to the lawman.

"Here, Cy, you better take this."

"Hell's bells!" breathed Cyrus. "It all happened — so damn *sudden*!"

"Get off of me and gimme my gun!" wailed the stranger. "Let me finish it! If I can't have her, I'd as soon be dead!" "He's drunk," Jake said in disgust. "Whiskey before noon — bad medicine."

"Ain't you ashamed, mister?" chided Stretch. "My buddy just now saved your doggone life."

"Who *asked* him to?" groaned the stranger. "Oh, hell! I don't wanta live no more . . . !"

"One drink too many," jeered Jake, "and he wants to blow his head off. And why? Because some female shut her door on him."

"You'll feel easier when you sober up," soothed Larry.

"It's worse when I'm sober!" gasped the stranger.

"Well, Cy, what're you waitin' for?" challenged Jake. "Do your duty. Don't you know suicide's against the law?"

"How would I know?" frowned Cyrus. "All the time I've been marshal of New Chance, I never once met a man that wanted to kill himself."

"You're supposed to lock him up so he can't try it again give him time to think it over," growled Jake. "And

12

check his pockets and take his belt. With a jack-knife he could cut his throat. With his belt he could hang himself."

"Think you can handle him, Cy?" asked Larry.

"If you need any help . . . " began Stretch.

"Be a sad day when I can't handle one crazy drunk," muttered Cyrus, ramming the pistol into his belt. He ordered Larry to rise, then bent to grasp an arm and haul the stranger to his feet. "C'mon, you. Don't give me no trouble and, after you've cooled off, maybe I'll feed you."

As the lawman began frogmarching him from the barroom, the stranger mumbled his speech of despair.

"Don't want to cool off — don't want to eat — only want to kill myself . . . "

Resenting this necessary but irksome chore, Cyrus Hindmarsh hustled his prisoner to the shabby log and clapboard building near the corner of Main and

Bonanza. The marshal's office and town jail had become his New Chance home since the Piper rooming house had closed up; he cooked his meals on the office stove and slept in a ground floor cell.

When had he last jailed a dangerous drunk? Months ago, long months ago. He glanced along the silent street before shoving the stranger across the threshold. Most of the original buildings still standing, but unoccupied. A too-quiet town, dying on its feet. He sighed mournfully, nudged his prisoner across to his untidy desk and ordered him to turn out his pockets.

"Then gimme your belt — *both belts.*"

"Both belts? How do I keep my pants up?"

"You should fret," sneered Cyrus. "You that's tired of livin'. Hey, what're you called?"

"Appleyard's my name," mumbled the stranger. "Edward Gwynn Appleyard."

The contents of his pockets didn't

add up to much. Eighty cents in small change, five paper dollars, a grubby kerchief, jack-knife, tobacco-sack, cigarette papers and matches. Cyrus frisked him carefully, took possession of his belts and warned him,

"I can't let you smoke. Crazy galoot like you — you're apt to set fire to a mattress, try and burn yourself to death. All right, Appleyard. Upstairs."

Moving groggily, still befuddled by whiskey, Ed Appleyard climbed to the upstairs cellblock with the marshal close behind. Cyrus installed him on the right side, a clean cell with a barred window through which the prisoner could look down on a goodly section of the main stem, if he could work up the energy to climb onto his bunk.

"You can see some of the town from there," he muttered, as he locked the cell-door. "And you ought to be real interested."

"I ain't interested in this burg,"

sighed Appleyard, "nor any other town."

"You ought to be interested," Cyrus insisted. "You and New Chance got somethin' in common."

"What?" frowned Appleyard.

"You hanker to die," scowled Cyrus. "Well, this town's dyin', and that's for sure. Been dyin' steady, ever since the pay-lodes petered out." He turned to leave, adding, "Enjoy your hangover."

"Thanks for nothin'," said Appleyard.

Descending to his office, Cyrus stowed the prisoner's personal effects in the safe. He reprimanded himself then. About to return to the Eureka and his checkers opponent, he suddenly remembered the routine.

"Out of practice," he reflected, dumping the file of Wanted bulletins on the desk, flopping into his swivel chair. "Been so long since I made an arrest — I'm gettin' careless — forgettin' procedures."

You take a stranger prisoner. You check the files. Never overlook the

16

possibility your man is wanted in some other territory.

He spent some 5 minutes leafing through the dodgers, then started convulsively, eyes bulging, jaw sagging.

"Hell's bells! Same hombre — nothin' surer!"

Stuffing the bulletin into his shirt, he sprang to his feet and dashed out, making for the Gazette office as fast as his legs could carry him. For the first time in a long time, he was running, and this unaccustomed exercise had the inevitable effect. He had to slow down, panting heavily, long before he reached the block in which the newspaper office was located.

During New Chance's boom years, the Gazette's editor and staff ran two editions off the pedal press every week. Nick Fleischer had prospered, though his tabloid's circulation was limited to the New Chance Pass area and a few outlying camps in the Rockies. Then, about the time the first company mines were closing down, Fleischer had gotten in the way of a wild bullet triggered by a likkered-up minehand. The town's only doctor, Todd Bayes, had done his utmost to save his patient. Fleischer hung on a whole week, conscious and in pain, appreciating Doc's efforts and proving his gratitude in a unique way.

"Nothing more you can do for me," he had said in the presence of reliable witnesses. "I don't believe I'm gonna make it, Doc. All I own is the Gazette and the building it's in. Got no relatives. Outlived them all. So, when I'm gone, you take over. You've been hanging around my office, admiring my equipment, talking of how you wished you'd studied journalism instead of medicine. The Gazette is your toy, old friend. Yours to play with in your spare time, you know?"

Those were the last coherent words uttered by the Gazette's founder. From full awareness, he sank into a coma some five hours later. And, by ironic coincidence, his grave in New Chance's Boot Hill was located close by that of

18

the miner whose bullet ended his life. One of Cyrus Hindmarsh's deputies, long since gone from the Pass, had cut short the miner's escape attempt with a well-aimed rifle-slug.

Nowadays, any local in need of Doc Bayes' professional services was more apt to find him at the Gazette office than around the Jubilee Road corner in his old surgery. The dwindling population stayed healthy — fortunately — while Doc experimented and tinkered with his pride and joy, the press, the type cases, paper and ink and all the other paraphernalia once used by the departed staff and his deceased benefactor. This special meeting had to be convened at the Gazette office for an obvious reason; the tubby medico was a member of the council and couldn't be lured away from his playthings.

Cyrus trudged in while Milo Tweedy, mayor of the town and owner of the New Chance Emporium, was holding forth. Nodding in doleful accord with his sentiments were Roscoe Lippert of the Eureka Saloon and Arnold Shell, owner of the New Chance Hotel. Maybe Doc was listening. Nobody could be sure about that, because he was happily fiddling with the press at this time.

"Listen, fellers . . ." began Cyrus.

"Don't interrupt!" chided the mayor. "Siddown and wait your turn, Cyrus!"

"Yeah, but . . ."

"Hold it down, Cy," growled Lippert. "What Milo's saying is important."

"Whole future of New Chance is in the balance," muttered Shell. "Stay quiet, Cy. Go on, Milo."

"Things aren't improvin'," declared Tweedy, pacing in agitation. "The situation's gettin' worse every day. What we got here is a dyin' town, by damn. And, unless we do somethin' about it, New Chance won't last another half-year. Stage passengers don't bring enough business to keep our heads above water. All three banks have quit, along with the other saloons, hotels, and stores. Next thing we know, Western Union'll quit and — where the hell's Jerry anyway? He's a councilman!"

"Five'll get you ten Jerry's tending his damn-blasted cabbage patch," scowled Lippert.

"Or his carrots," Shell said scornfully.

"If Western Union quits, we'll have no way of stayin' in touch with any other town," complained Tweedy, "except through the Philby Stage Line."

"Milo, the Philby line won't de-route its east-west services," Doc assured him, still fiddling with the pedal press. "They have to come through the pass. Easiest route to and from Santa Fe. How else could they get through the mountains?"

"Will you, for pity's sakes, quit messin' with that contraption and pay attention?" scowled the mayor. "Hell, Doc, we got an emergency on our hands . . . !"

"I'm listening," shrugged Doc.

"We're losin' money every week

21

since the miners pulled out," declared Tweedy. "Losin' our people, our trade, our only chance to keep this town alive."

New Chance's civic leaders were a mixed quartet, a study in contrasts, but united by a common bond. Doc Bayes was the most placid. Well, he could afford to be. A confirmed bachelor with no nagging wife to plague him, he had time on his hands nowadays, time to dream his dreams, seeing himself as a frontier newspaperman. Twice in the past five weeks, he had set up, printed and issued special editions of the Gazette. The news content had been meagre, but Doc was proving his point; given the equipment, he could put out a paper.

Roscoe Lippert, also a bachelor, was typical of his class, the gambler-turned-saloonkeeper. Lean, saturnine and well-groomed, he had kept the Eureka operating at a profit until the boom fizzled out, and now he shared his cronies' mounting alarm. He had

22

a stake in New Chance's future — if New Chance had a future.

The discussion continued, Lippert interjecting an opinion whenever the scrawny mayor or the moon-faced, balding hotel-keeper paused to catch their breath. Doc and Cyrus had heard it all before, Milo Tweedy bemoaning the drop in trade, Arnold Shell sourly complaining of all the vacant rooms in his hotel. They wrangled, and the wrangling was futile, little more than an outlet for their mercenary emotions; they were businessmen after all.

"We're gettin' nowhere with all this back-talk!" Tweedy was becoming edgy, his temper on a loose rein. "Damnitall, what we need is an idea, somethin' positive. How do we breathe life back into a town like New Chance? Somebody tell me *that*!"

"Can I tell you about . . . ?" began Cyrus.

"Will you butt outa this, consarn you?" raged Tweedy.

"Hush up, Cy," chided Shell. "Hey,

Doc, what do you say?"

"All I know is we won't lose the stage line," muttered Doc. "They can't run an east-west service unless they continue to use the regular mountain route — which cuts through this pass."

"You're a lot of help, I don't think," growled Tweedy. "The Philby outfit could keep operation with just the stage depot, a barn and the waterholes. We're tryin' to figure how to keep this whole town alive. Not just Oley Craydon's office, Doc. The whole town."

"A gold strike put New Chance on the map," said Doc, turning at last from his beloved press. He squatted on the edge of the desk once used by Nick Fleischer and began filling his pipe. "Well, I guess it's too much to hope another party of prospectors finds a new pay-vein somewhere close to our town."

"They dug up all the country hereabouts — like a pack of gophers — before they quit," sighed Shell. "No, we can't count on another gold strike."

"Maybe if we could encourage home-steaders, farmers, ranchers," suggested Lippert.

"Good graze on the flats west of the mountains," shrugged Tweedy. "But that area's a long trace from the pass. If cattlemen came, they'd more likely build their own town."

"How about sheep?" demanded Shell. "Sheep breed like rabbits in mountain country — I think."

"Sheepmen are mighty close with buck," said Lippert, grimacing. "Not the kind to risk their coin on games of chance."

"If New Chance could become a shrine," mused Doc, as he lit his pipe.

"A what?" frowned Tweedy.

"A shrine," said Doc. "You know what I mean, Milo. Some important identity — like Governor Lew Wallace for instance — pays New Chance an official visit, becomes ill and obligingly dies here. We bury him in our local cemetery and New Chance becomes a memorial, the town where the territorial governor cashed in his chips. Tourists would make the pilgrimage from all compass-points to see the last resting place of a man who made history."

"If we knew he was feelin' poorly, we could invite him up here," Tweedy suggested, but half-heartedly, "and hope for the worst. Well, Doc? How much d'you know about Lew Wallace's health?"

"He's hale and hearty," said Doc.

"You're a lot of help, I don't think," mumbled Tweedy.

"Last I heard of the governor, he was writing a book," shrugged Doc. "His personal physician is an old college pal of mine. I had a letter from him last winter. He said the governor's all caught up with his scribbling. Something biblical. He's gonna call it — let me think now. Uh huh. Yeah. Ben Something-Or-Other. Yeah, now I remember. Ben Hur."

"We'll need something better than

a story-writing governor who could outlive us all," opined Lippert. "We need a miracle."

Cyrus coughed impatiently. Tweedy glowered at him.

"Are you still here?"

"Don't mind me," Cyrus said resentfully. "I'm just your town marshal — here on law business."

"All right, Cy, go ahead." Shell eyed his colleagues boredly. "We aren't solving our problem, no matter how much we talk about it. So we might's well give our marshal a few minutes."

"Say your piece, Cyrus," scowled Tweedy. "But it better be important."

"Well, it's about Billy Reese," said Cyrus. "I guess you've heard of him . . . "

"All New Mexico knows that thievin', trigger-happy, kill-crazy renegade," muttered Tweedy. "Arizona and Colorado too."

"Bloodthirstiest bandit of them all, the newspapers called him," said Lippert. "Warrants for him — a price on his

27

head — clear from Denver to the west coast."

"He was even wanted right here in New Chance, as I recall," frowned Shell.

"That's a fact," nodded Cyrus. "He pumped four slugs into a prospector and made off with his little sack of nuggets. And there were witnesses."

"Well, that was a long time back," shrugged Lippert. "I haven't heard talk of Billy Reese in three years or more."

Cyrus produced the bulletin and offered it to Tweedy.

"I had to arrest a feller just now," he reported. "Got him locked snug in a cell. He calls himself Ed Appleyard — but I think he's Billy Reese."

2

Drastic Measures

THE scrawny marshal was suddenly a mighty popular law-man. His announcement won an ovation from Tweedy, Shell and Lippert, who pounded his back, pumped his hand and earnestly congratulated him, while Doc Bayes puffed on his pipe and warily studied the pen portrait of the notorious outlaw re-produced on the bulletin.

"Right when we most needed it!" cried the mayor. "Right when New Chance was on its knees — near finished — Cyrus came through for us!"

"Think of it!" chuckled Shell. "Reese is more famous than Sam Bass or Wes Hardin! He's had as much publicity in the big city newspapers as Bill Cody or Hickok! And he's been nailed at

29

last — right here in New Chance — by our marshal!"

"This is a proud day for our town, Cyrus," declared Lippert. "We won't forget you for this."

"Uh — listen," frowned Cyrus. "It ain't like you think. I didn't have to fight him. Plain truth is he tried to shoot himself in Roscoe's saloon and one of them Texans stopped him 'fore he could pull trigger, and then I took him to jail."

"Billy Reese, plagued by remorse, tried to cheat the gallows by committing suicide," Lippert said ponderously. "How about *that*, Doc? Now *there*'s a story you could write."

"And publish," insisted Tweedy. "Why, sure! A special edition of the Gazette! We'll send copies to all the San Francisco dailies . . . !"

"Chicago — and New York," grinned Shell.

"Cyrus said there's a warrant for him in our territory," Tweedy reminded them. "By damn! You realize what that means? We can hold the trial — and hang him — in New Chance! There'll be people flockin' here from all over the country — reporters from all the big papers . . . !"

"Before you have Jerry Webb wire the circuit-judge, there's a point we oughtn't overlook," Doc interjected dryly. "Little matter of positive identification."

"We got us a professional lawman here, Doc, with a trained eye," asserted Tweedy. "Marshal Hindmarsh's word is good enough for me. If he says this feller is Billy Reese . . . "

"He sure looks like the feller on the bulletin," said Cyrus. "A dead ringer."

"We ought to go take a look at him anyway," suggested Shell.

"Yeah — especially Doc." Lippert stared hard at the medico and remarked to his cronies. "We're all forgetting something, boys. Only one of us ever saw Billy up close — and that one is Doc."

"By damn," frowned Tweedy. "I got so excited — I *did* forget."

"That was an experience I'd like to forget, but probably never will," Doc soberly assured them.

"Around four years ago, wasn't it?" prodded Tweedy.

"About four and a half years," said Doc. "I had a practice up in Tannerville, Colorado."

"Reese made you dig a bullet out of him, as I recall," said Shell. "Stayed conscious the whole time."

"The only occasion on which I've performed surgery — with the patient prodding me with a cocked six-gun," said Doc. "Oh, yes, I have good cause to remember Bloody Billy."

"That incident should be included in your story," offered Shell. "As they say in the newspaper business, it'd make great copy."

"Doc's identification will be the clincher," declared Lippert, rising from his chair. "So what're we waiting for?"

The town council moved from the Gazette office to the town jail in double-quick time, collecting the other two councilmen en route. Oley Craydon emerged from the Eureka, disgruntled that Cyrus hadn't returned to the saloon to continue their checkers game, and was promptly carried along, Lippert and Shell linking arms with him and muttering an explanation. Jerry Webb, the town's pudgy, amiable telegrapher, was plucked out of his potato patch by Tweedy to join the party, still hefting a hand-fork.

They followed the marshal into his office and up the stairs to the cellblock. And there, with Cyrus on guard with a cocked .45 and Tweedy and his cohorts watching intently, Doc squatted beside the prisoner on the bunk and subjected him to a careful scrutiny.

"Well, Doc, what d'you say?" demanded Tweedy.

"Like Cyrus said — a dead ringer," frowned Doc.

"Listen, gents, you got me curious."

33

Cold sober and soreheaded, Appleyard eyed them perplexedly. "What's this all about, huh?"

"As if you don't know," chuckled Shell.

"That's right," nodded Appleyard. "I dunno."

"No use denyin' it, Reese!" growled Tweedy, scowling ferociously. "We all know you!"

"What'd he call me?" Appleyard asked Doc.

"Reese," said Doc. "They believe you're Billy Reese."

"Great day in the mornin'!" gasped Appleyard. "You mean — Billy Reese the outlaw?"

"We sure don't mean Billy Reese the Sunday school teacher," leered Oley Craydon.

"You're Reese, by damn!" accused Tweedy. "And we're gonna hang you — on a special-built gallows!"

"Bonanza Road would be the best site for a gallows," opined Shell. "Just around the corner from the jailhouse.

34

We could have benches and chairs for the out-of-towners, rig platforms for the overflow crowd. Quite an event it'll be."

"We're gonna make *history*!" announced Tweedy.

"Well — uh — I'd sure like to oblige you gents," shrugged Appleyard. "And I wouldn't mind hangin' on accounta I was fixin' to kill myself anyway. Just as soon have somebody do the job for me. But I ain't who you think I am. I'm Ed Appleyard and, in my whole life, I never killed anybody nor robbed a bank or a stagecoach and that's the ever-lovin' truth."

"Pull your shirt up," ordered Doc.

"Uh — what . . . ?" began Appleyard.

"The left side," said Doc.

"Do as you're told!" barked Tweedy.

Nervously, the prisoner tugged his shirt from his pants.

"Now the undershirt," Doc said impatiently.

Appleyard obeyed. The medico briefly studied the area between the left hip and armpit, then rose and quit the cell.

"Well, what about . . . ?" began Tweedy.

"Downstairs," said Doc.

Cyrus re-secured the door and, with Doc leading, the town council moved along the passage and descended to the office. They eyed the medico expectantly, while he filled his pipe again.

"Forget it," he said bluntly, as he scratched a match. He held the name to the fresh tobacco, puffed the brier to life and shook his head. "I agree there's a striking resemblance, but the man is not Reese, and that's that."

"Aw, c'mon now, Doc!" protested Tweedy. "You could be mistaken, couldn't you?"

"Not a chance," said Doc. "I extracted a bullet from between his ribs — meaning Billy Reese. The wound had to be stitched and . . ."

"What were you looking for? A scar?" challenged Lippert.

"Scars heal," offered Craydon.

"Why, sure," nodded Webb. "Given time."

"Stop grasping at straws," chided Doc. "The scar could heal, certainly. But it couldn't *disappear*. New skin won't grow over the kind of surgery I had to perform on that damn killer. The man upstairs has never suffered a wound on that side of his torso. You just have to accept it, boys. He's not Billy Reese."

"But he's *gotta* be!" wailed Tweedy.

"Well, damnitall, he's still our prisoner," blustered Shell. "And he claims he wants to die, doesn't he?"

"That's what he said!" Tweedy nodded eagerly. "We all heard him!"

"So who's to know he's not the real Billy?" challenged the hotelkeeper. "We could still spread the word, tell the whole country we've got Billy Reese in our jail and we're gonna try him and hang him."

"Sounds reasonable to me," frowned Craydon.

"Mightn't be one hundred percent legal," mused Cyrus. "But what the hell?"

"I mean — everybody dies," shrugged Craydon. "This Appleyard feller tried to blow his brains out a little while ago, so it won't be any skin off his nose, will it?"

"I'm — uh — not quite sure . . ." began Webb.

"There'll be no backin' down, Jerry," growled Tweedy. "We already agreed this is the best chance we'll ever get to make New Chance famous . . . "

"A town as historically significant as Tombstone, Virginia City, Dodge or Deadwood," Lippert said a trifle pompously. "Think about it. Deadwood, for instance, will never be forgotten, because Wild Bill Hickok was assassinated there."

"Yeah, sure, Roscoe, you've made your point," nodded Shell.

"I tell you, the old town would be reborn!" enthused Tweedy. "We could open up the Talbot House, the

38

Rialto and a couple other hotels to accommodate the visitors . . . "

"Sell souvenirs to the tourists," grinned Shell.

"Oughta be some kind of monument over Billy's grave," suggested Craydon.

"If head office ever found out . . ." fretted the telegrapher.

"Will you for the love of Mike quit quibblin'?" chided Tweedy. "Look, Jerry, it's gonna be our secret. Nobody else'll know, so how can any of us get in trouble? It's a perfect plan — fool-proof — so long as we all go along with it and keep our mouths shut."

"We ought to swear a pact here and now," suggested Lippert.

"I'm puttin' it to the vote," said Tweedy. "All in favor of New Chance grabbin' this last chance to put New Chance on the map — reporters and photographers flockin' in to write stories and take pictures — trade boomin' again — raise your right hands."

Shell, Lippert, Cyrus, Craydon and Webb imitated Tweedy's action, lifting their right hands. All eyes then focussed on Doc, who had sagged into a chair. His pipe had gone cold. He was eyeing his old cronies incredulously, as though seeing them for the first time.

"Now, Doc, don't hold out on us," chided Shell. "It has to be a unanimous vote."

"Hell, you've seen many a man die," Tweedy reminded him. "What difference if Appleyard hangs as Billy Reese? If somebody hadn't stopped him in the Eureka, he'd have blown his fool head off and Oley would be layin' him out now, fittin' him for a pine box."

Doc was silent a long moment. Then, shaking his head, he softly declared,

"I don't believe it. I've heard everything you mercenary ghouls have said — and I don't believe it. It's fantastic, far-fetched, bizarre . . ."

"Hey, that's an idea," interjected Craydon. "We could have a bazaar, sell trinkets and stuff — salt-water taffy and ice cream — rig a shootin' gallery — raffle little pieces of cotton cut from

Reese's clothes . . . "

"Shuddup, Oley," frowned Lippert. "Doc, what's the matter with you?"

"What's the matter with *me*?" gasped Doc. "Better I should ask what's the matter with you — all of you! Are you out of your profit-counting minds? You can't just — try and hang an impostor . . . !"

"He'll be a *voluntary* impostor," countered Shell. "Damnit, Doc, it's not as if we're hanging him against his will."

"In other words, when this poor no-account turned suicidal, he presented you with a golden opportunity," Doc said scathingly.

"Why, certainly," nodded Tweedy. "And we aim to take advantage of it."

"Conveniently disregarding the ethics of the thing," accused Doc. "Committing a fraud of — of monumental proportions!"

"The monument could be Homer Beechley's chore," mused Webb. "When it comes to stone masonry, Homer's a real artist."

"Great balls of fire!" Doc clapped a hand to his brow. "You've got him tried, convicted and executed already — and buried under a monument! It's like a — a nightmare . . . !"

For almost a quarter-hour Tweedy and his cohorts worked on the medico, bullying, wheedling, wrangling. And then, in a moment of inspiration, Roscoe Lippert struck with deadly aim at the medico's Achilles' heel. What of Doc's long-cherished ambition? Here, surely, was Doc's own golden opportunity. Big city journalists, maybe a dozen or more, would converge on New Chance to cover the trial, but it would be Tod Bayes, physician-turned-newspaperman, who started the ball rolling. Doc would break the story and become the centre of attention, envied by veteran scribes from the widely-circulating tabloids of Chicago, New York and the west coast. Could Doc ignore this once-in-a-lifetime chance?

Fame. Adulation. Recognition of his journalistic genius.

Doc haggled, loath to abandon his professional ethics. There would have to be a compromise, he insisted.

"I'll go along, but only up to a point," he announced. "We'll make capital of your wild scheme, with Appleyard's co-operation. We'll circulate our claim that Billy Reese has been captured in New Chance and will stand trial here. Every wild lie you money-grubbing rogues have dreamed up — I'll condone and support."

"But you're making a condition?" prodded Lippert.

"That's right," said Doc, nodding vehemently. "And you'll agree to that condition or, by Godfrey, you can forget the whole thing."

"Well — uh — what's your condition?" demanded Shell.

"No hanging," said Doc.

"But — damnitall . . . !" began Tweedy.

"That's going too far, Milo," growled

Doc. "We can't take a human life, publicly execute an innocent man — even with his consent. It's too damn ridiculous, not to mention illegal."

"But the hanging will be the high spot of the whole deal," protested Shell.

"All them visitors," frowned Cyrus. "They're gonna be plumb disappointed, if we don't go ahead with the hangin'."

"There's a handy alternative," Doc pointed out. "What could be more sensational than hanging Billy Reese in New Chance?"

"Notin'," scowled Tweedy. "He has to hang."

"You got a better idea, Doc?" asked Craydon.

"What're we gonna do?" frowned Webb. "Let this feller commit suicide — kill himself in his cell — after the trial?"

"Better than that — far better," declared Doc. "He's going to escape."

"Escape? Hell!" groaned Tweedy.

"He stands trial, is found guilty and

44

sentenced to hang," said Doc. "And then he escapes — mysteriously! No logical explanation. That, my friends, would be a *real* sensation! And, when it's all over, our conscience would be clear. No blood on our hands. We'd still reap the benefit of the publicity. We'd still be famous."

"I don't like it," said Tweedy. "We'd be a laughing stock. Folks'd say New Chance didn't have what it takes to hold a convicted killer."

"It wouldn't look good for me," complained Cyrus.

"I'd like it better if Billy got shot while tryin' to escape," said Tweedy.

"Forget it," Doc said curtly. "We do it my way, or not at all. And that's my final word."

"Doc's got us over a barrel," frowned Lippert. "We have no choice, Milo."

"All in favor we do it Doc's way," sighed Tweedy.

This time, the vote was unanimous. There in Cyrus Hindarsh's poky office, the wild scheme was devised and set into motion. The prisoner was interviewed again and advised of the council's decision, every far-fetched detail — with one exception. Nothing was said about Doc's all-important proviso, the fact that Appleyard's escape and disappearance would be organized — somehow — at some as yet undecided time after the trial.

"I sure appreciate this, gents." He thanked them humbly. "You'll be savin' me the trouble of killin' myself and I'll be dyin' famous."

"Remember now, Ed," cautioned Lippert. "Secrecy! This is just between you and us, understand? If the truth ever leaked out . . . "

"Don't you fret, mister," mumbled Appleyard. "When them newspaper-fellers asks their questions, I'll do right by you. I'll make like I'm Billy Reese himself."

"Just one last point," suggested Shell. "From now on, we'd better get into the habit of calling him 'Billy'. Can't afford any slip-ups."

"That's an easy name to remember," shrugged the prisoner. "I'm Billy Reese, and I won't forget — if you don't."

"Maybe it's unimportant, but I'll ask anyway," frowned Doc. "Why are you so eager to commit suicide, young feller?"

"I ain't so young," said Appleyard. "I'm thirty-two."

"About the same age as Bloody Billy!" chuckled Craydon.

"My girl ran off with a lousy cardsharp that rigs himself in fancy clothes and greases his hair with pomade," Appleyard said solemnly, "and I'll just never get over it. I just gotta die, on accounta the hurt is more'n I can live with."

As they descended from the cellblock, Doc muttered a warning to Cyrus.

"Watch him carefully. Any man who'd want to kill himself — because of a woman — is a special kind of idiot."

They separated outside the jail, Jerry Webb hustling to his office to wire the big news to Denver, Doc making for the Gazette office at a brisk trot, Shell returning to the New Chance Hotel, Tweedy to his store, Craydon and Lippert to the Eureka Saloon.

Within the quarter-hour, the half-alive town high in the Rockies was buzzing with excitement, and the excitement was reaching further afield. Webb wired Santa Fe and Albuquerque and, for good measure, Brampton, Utah and San Ernesto, Arizona, after he was through with the Denver operator. By mid-afternoon or that day, type was being set up for special editions in every town contacted by busy Jerry Webb.

But the report destined to carry the greatest impact was written by Doc Bayes. The Gazette's account of the capture of Billy Reese was circulating at 9 o'clock the following morning, Doc having spent the night setting type and working his press. A dozen copies were picked up by the westbound Philby stage a half-hour later and, watching the coach roll away from the depot, Doc savored the heady champagne of success. He had done it. His story would be duplicated in scores of frontier newspapers, embroidered, exaggerated maybe, and circulating clear to the Sierra Nevada and beyond, far north of the Humboldt, east of the Mississippi, south of the Rio Grande.

Not until they were working their way through a late breakfast in the dining room of the New Chance Hotel did Larry and Stretch get to analyze the aftermath of yesterday's incident in the Eureka barroom. Breakfast was served them by the comely Molly Lamont, niece of Arnold and Sadie Shell and the town's prettiest spinster. Her smile was radiant and, to the observant Texans, it seemed her blue eyes and rosy cheeks had an extra glow this morning.

"Biggest thing that's happened to New Chance since the first gold strike," she announced, as she set the laden tray down. "Eat hearty, gentlemen, and read all about it."

"Molly, I didn't know your local paper was still in business," drawled Larry, unfolding the special edition.

"Doc Bayes inherited it," she explained. "Seems journalism was his secret dream, kind of, and when Mister Fleischer died and left him the Gazette . . ."

"Well, we won't hold it against him," shrugged Stretch. "We ain't real partial to scribblers, Molly. But this one's a sawbones as well, which means he's got an honest profession."

"Uncle Arnie's walking on air," she confided. "Mayor Tweedy's wearing his Sunday suit and Mister Craydon's about to paint the stage depot and the marshal's office. It'll be a proud day for New Chance when that terrible outlaw stands trial. Be folks traveling here from all over. Reporters — tourists . . ."

She hurried away to the kitchen, leaving the drifters to start on their ham and eggs. With his mouth half-full, Stretch mumbled,

"I don't read as smart as you, so you

50

tell me what it says." Larry munched and swallowed while scanning the front page. He began reading and, studying him covertly, Stretch noted his changing expressions, surprise giving way to amusement, the grimace of resentment quickly replaced by a good-humored grin.

"We're gonna shake Doc's hand," he drawled, discarding the paper and returning to his breakfast. "He's done us a favor."

"How come?" demanded Stretch.

"The feller at Lippert's, him that tried to shoot himself," said Larry. "It turns out he's an owlhooter with a price on his head. Name of Billy Reese. Wanted all over, includin' right here in New Chance."

"I'll be a sonofa Comanche," frowned Stretch. "You done captured an outlaw — and didn't know it."

"The way Doc writes it, I wasn't even there," grinned Larry. "He don't even name us. And I wouldn't have it any other way."

"Howzat again?" blinked Stretch.

"Doc gives all the credit to Hindmarsh, the badge-toter," shrugged Larry. "Makes it read like Hindmarsh recognized this Reese, challenged him and got the drop on him."

"That's a lotta hogwash," protested Stretch.

"Yup," agreed Larry. "But better for us. Let Hindmarsh have the glory. Do we want our names in the newspapers?"

"We've been in too many newspapers," Stretch said bitterly. "Who needs a big reputation?"

Molly's uncle entered the dining room and, after a moment of hesitation, came across to the Texans' table.

"You've read the story," he guessed. "Well now, Mister Valentine, I don't blame you for resenting the way we — uh — kind of juggled the facts of Reese's capture. But if you'll try and see it our way, we'd certainly appreciate your cooperation."

"I like it the way it is," Larry calmly informed him.

52

"It just happens my buddy and me ain't partial to . . . " began Stretch.

"Publicity?" prodded Shell.

"That's the word," nodded Stretch.

"So Marshal Hindmarsh is welcome to the glory," said Larry.

"And you won't let on?" Shell asked hopefully. "I mean, when the reporters arrive? It means a great deal to us, Mister Valentine. A new start for New Chance. A lot of visitors. More business . . . "

"We're good at keepin' our mouths shut," said Larry.

"That's mighty decent of you," Shell acknowledged. "And I'm speaking for Mayor Tweedy and the whole town council."

The Texans nodded affably as Shell hurried away. Resuming their breakfast they traded comments and opinions. Should they check out of their comfortable room in this hotel, saddle up and quit New Chance? Constantly seeking in safe retreat where the pace of life was slow, they saw New Chance as an ideal haven for a couple of battle-weary trouble-shooters. Now that the would-be suicide had been identified as the infamous Billy Reese, the pace would quicken; New Chance would be a hive of activity a few days from now.

"So maybe we ought to move on?" asked Stretch.

"So maybe we ought to stay put," countered Larry.

"Well . . . " The taller Texan shrugged nonchalantly. "Whatever you say is okay by me."

"The town'll get lively," Larry predicted. "But all the visitors, the reporters and such, they'll be too busy with the trial, too caught up in writin' their lies and takin' pictures too busy to notice a couple peace-lovin' Texans."

"We'd be lost in the shuffle, huh?" prodded Stretch.

"A feller once said it's easy to hide in a crowd," drawled Larry. "And New Chance is gonna be mighty crowded."

By noon of the following day,

representatives of several big city dailies were packing their grips to begin the journey to the transit town in the New Mexico Rockies.

And other interested parties were reacting in various ways, for personal and venal reasons, to the news of Billy Reese's capture.

3

Buzzards and Wolves

IN Albuquerque, the buzzards.
Sharing a table in that town's
lowliest and dingiest bar, Nils
Mulder and his three shabby cohorts
read the local editor's version of the
Reese arrest and compared notes.
Bounty-hunting was their game and,
like many of that breed, they were short
on scruples and long on greed. They
worked as a team, their leader being
keenly devoted to his own welfare,
believing in safety in numbers.

Having read the report, Mulder
delved into his tattered jacket for his
grubby, dog-eared notebook and began
leafing through it.

"Let's see now. Billy Reese. Well,
hell! Five thousand they're offerin' for
him in Pennant Butte, Arizona." He

surveyed his cronies from under shaggy brows and scratched his bulbous nose. Broad-featured and thickset, he was the ugliest member of the unsavory quartet. "They're holdin' him in this two-bit burg — New Chance — up in the mountains. And he ain't worth a dime to us there."

"That what it says in your ledger, Mulder?" challenged Purvis, the dude of the group. "Better check it again."

"There's a warrant for him in New Chance," muttered Mulder. "It still holds good, but nobody in that burg got around to postin' bounty on him."

Purvis stroked his mustache and toyed with his cravat-pin, an imitation diamond. In the matter of looks, he was almost as unprepossessing as his leader, but he fancied himself as a rake and a womanizer, irresistible in fact. And there were other touches just as phoney as his stickpin. The striped suit had been tailored for somebody else; Purvis had stolen it. The material of the fancy vest was cheap and, in his hip pocket, he always toted his 'come-on wad' — a 2-inch thick fold of paper cut to the size of banknotes, the outer 'show-bill' a genuine $50. By flashing this wad at the right moment, Purvis claimed he could have any woman of his choice.

"New Chance is no two-bit burg," he frowned. "Last I heard it was boomin'."

"I got good information — *always* got good information," leered Mulder. "No gold there any more. The mines were all worked out. It's a half-alive town now."

"They got Reese in their jail," mused Dall, a lean rogue with a nervous squint, "and they plan on holdin' him for trial."

"Better he should be tried in Pennant Butte, amigos." Ortero, the swarthy Mexican, bared buck teeth in a knowing grin. He had thrown in with Mulder and his cronies after fleeing north from Sonora, dismissed by the law authorities of his homeland for repeated acts of cowardice. "Five thousand we collect in Pennant Butte." He dilated his eyes and licked his thick lips. "Mucho dinero!"

"They want him alive in Pennant Butte," said Mulder, stowing his notebook away. "Well, I reckon we can handle it. All we got to do is bust him out of the New Chance calaboose and head west through the high country. We could make the Butte in three-four days."

"Mightn't be all that easy," warned Dall.

"Quit your frettin'," chided Mulder. "There's always an angle." Abruptly, he got to his feet. "Better get started. I calculate we got about seventy-five miles of hard ridin' ahead of us, if we travel straight northwest. Like I always say, a straight line is the fastest route."

As they moved out into Albuquerque's main street, Purvis set his hat at a jaunty angle and remarked,

"There better be a purty woman or

two in New Chance. Money ain't all I crave."

* * *

In Santa Fe, the wolves.

Three members of the original Reese gang had roosted in the big town these past two years, digging a niche for themselves, changing their names and avoiding the curiosity of the local lawmen; few of Reese's old minions were on record in any sheriff's office.

While the burly Nate Rocklin polished glasses behind the bar of the Ace Of Diamonds Saloon, Silky Weems lounged in a chair by the side wall, re-reading the lead story in the current edition of the Santa Fe Post. Saturnine, well-groomed and an expert cardsharp, he had made expenses in the local gambling houses, usually winning enough to keep himself in expensive Havanas, fine food and top grade bourbon. But other gamblers had eyed him askance of late. His days in

60

Santa Fe were numbered; that was the thought in his mind when he seated himself and picked up the discarded newspaper.

Obeying the gambler's gesture, Rocklin nodded to the second barkeep.

"Take over for a while, Benny."

He trudged to where Weems sat and pulled up a chair.

"What's up?"

"He's not dead," Weems said quietly.

"Who's not dead?" demanded Rocklin. "Hey! You don't mean . . . ?"

"Speak softly, Nate," chided Weems. "If anybody suspected we'd ridden with that sadistic sonofabitch, there'd be tin stars climbing all over us."

"He's *gotta* be dead!" hissed Rocklin. "We saw that shack blown to little bits!"

"But we never found his body."

"What's to find? The blast splintered the shingles, blew the stove forty feet up the hillside. So there'd be nothin' left of his mangy carcass."

"Ever hear of a place called New

61

Chance? It's a pass up in the Rockies. Their marshal arrested a man and identified him as you-know-who, and they plan on holding a trial there — hanging him."

"He couldn't be . . . !"

"We have to make sure, Nate. If it's Reese, we'll figure some way of breaking him out."

"Make him *our* prisoner, huh?"

"Right. Take him someplace quiet and then work on him, give him some of his own medicine." The gambler's eyes gleamed; his voice dropped to little more than a whisper. "He always enjoyed inflicting pain."

"Give me five minutes with that polecat and I'll loosen his tongue," Rocklin grimly vowed. "He'll talk, I guarantee."

"But we won't take his word for it," muttered Weems. "We'll make him lead us to wherever he cached it — the coin, the gold, the paper money we helped him steal."

"Damn him to hell," breathed

62

Rocklin. "That last share-out — just nickels and dimes. He tricked us, ran out on us . . . " He paused, eyeing Weems uncertainly. "Silky, this galoot in the New Chance jail just *couldn't* be him. We're wishin' out loud and you know it. No man could get away alive from that shack. The blast — after we set it afire to faze him out . . . "

"There'll always be a doubt — unless we make sure," shrugged Weems. "That's what it gets down to, Nate."

"You sayin' we're gonna head back to the Arido Hills — to take another look?" challenged Rocklin.

"There's no other way," Weems said firmly. "We're going back to where it ended — or where we *think* it ended. And if we find anything, some indication Reese could've escaped before the explosion, we'll travel on to New Chance — and do what has to be done."

"What about the others?" demanded Rocklin.

"We'll need every man we can find,"

63

said Weems. "This jail-break — if it comes to that — will be a big operation."

"Dacey'll come along," opined Rocklin. "He's kind of chicken-livered, but what the hell? If he wants his share of Reese's pile, he'll have to work for it just like the rest of us."

"It shouldn't take more than an hour for you to tell Keeler you're quitting, collect what's due to you, collect Grose and saddle up," said Weems. "Meanwhile I'll be buying provisions. As for Jardine and the others, I know where to find them. We can pick them up on the way north to the hills."

"They still camped along Gila Creek?" asked Rocklin.

"Afraid to show their faces after that debacle at Verde City," said Weems, grinning contemptuously. "Well, I warned them against trying a bank job — without me along to plan every move."

"Whole deal blew up in their faces,"

recalled Rocklin. "I dunno how they out-ran that posse."

"They've laid low ever since," said Weems. "Safe enough to deal them in, I'd say. It could be a chore for the whole outfit anyway, Nate. They all have a stake in it." He folded the newspaper, stowed it in a pocket and rose from his chair. "Pack your gear and settle with your boss. I'll meet you and Grose in an hour, north end of town."

"We'll be there," Rocklin assured him.

They rendezvoused on schedule, Weems well-mounted on a high-stepping black gelding, a duster protecting his expensive town clothes, a sack of provisions slung from his saddlehorn. Also toting supplies were Rocklin and the thin, shifty-eyed Dacey Grose, the most nervous member of the old Reese gang. It was typical of Grose that, during his stay in Santa Fe, he had been content to work at menial chores; he was tending a manure heap

65

behind a livery stable when Rocklin collected him.

As they began the first phase of their northward journey, Grose eyed the gambler sidelong, grimaced uneasily and declared,

"If Billy *is* alive, I'm just as glad he ain't on the loose."

"Feel that much safer, do you?" accused Weems. "Knowing he's in jail?"

"Dacey was always the jumpy one," chuckled Rocklin. "Remember how he used to say Billy wasn't human, and how Billy could look into a man's brain and see what he's thinkin'?"

"Billy ain't like ordinary men," mumbled Grose.

"He's not all that different," Weems said harshly. "He'll bleed like any other man bleeds — I promise you."

"There you go again," frowned Rocklin. "We saw him blowed sky-high, but you already decided he's alive."

"We saw the shack blown sky-high,"

countered Weems. "But now we can't be certain he was in it at the time of the blast."

"I wonder what it was," said Grose. "Dynamite or blastin' powder?"

"One or the other," shrugged Rocklin. "Must've been prospectors usin' the place to stash their gear. Billy didn't know it when he took cover there, and we didn't know it — else we wouldn't have tried to burn him out of there."

"All these years I've assumed the cash was destroyed along with Reese," declared Weems. "Now — I'm not so sure."

In the late afternoon they reached the camp on the near bank of Gila Creek. Weems easily located the spot. A campfire was hastily smothered when they rounded a bend of the trail running level with the waterway, a sure indication Jardine and his pals were still in fear of law-posses. He rose in his saddle and called a reassurance.

"Light it up again, Harp! You've nothing to fear from us!"

They reined up and listened. After a slight pause, they heard the familiar clicking sounds. Guns were being uncocked and a gruff voice challenging them cautiously.

"Silky — Rocky . . . ?"

"And Grose," grinned Rocklin. "Take it easy, Harp. The old outfit's all together again."

"Keep a' comin'! Hey! You bring any booze?"

"I knew he'd ask that," scowled Weems, as they continued their advance. "Harp Jardine and his damn thirst."

When they rode into the semi-circle of rocks in sight of the creek-bank, George Earl was scooping dirt and ash away from the still-smoldering embers of the fire, throwing on fresh kindling to get it blazing again. Karl Sturm was hunkered by the picketed horses, his rifle across his knees and his hawk-like visage creased in a wry grin. As florid as ever, stubbled, unkempt and unwashed, Harp Jardine stepped forward to offer his hand, as Weems and his companions dismounted.

"Good to see you, Silky. Still the dude, huh? Hey, George, Karl, get an eyeful of Silky's fancy rig."

"Unpack your gear," offered Earl. "I'll have supper ready in a little while."

"We won't be staying," Weems announced, after shaking Jardine's hand. "If we get moving as soon as we've eaten, we'll reach the hills that much faster. And, believe me, there's good reason for haste."

"What's Silky talkin' about?" Sturm asked Rocklin.

"What hills?" demanded Earl.

"Forgotten, have you, George?" growled Rocklin. "North a ways. The Arido Hills. Last place we ever saw Billy."

"That double-crossin' skunk." Jardine spat in disgust. "When he got blowed to little stinkin' bits, we lost our only chance to get our hands on what's rightly ours." He turned to Weems, gesturing angrily. "You ever think about it, Silky? If he had all the loot with him, it burned along with him. And, if it was cached someplace, only he knew about it. Far as we're concerned, it's lost for all time."

"Maybe," said Weems.

"What d'you mean — maybe?" challenged Jardine.

"Read this," ordered Weems, producing the newspaper. "And, to save time, read it aloud. That'll save repeating it all to George and Karl."

Squatting in the fire-glow, Harp Jardine read aloud from the front page report in the Santa Fe Post with Earl and Sturm hovering close, interrupting at frequent intervals with earblistering profanity. Earl then bestirred himself and resumed cooking supper.

The situation was discussed, but not debated, during that meal by the creek-bank. There could be no argument as to the next move to be made by Billy Reese's one-time followers. If, by some strange quirk of fate, the wrong man was filling a cell in the

70

New Chance jail, they had only one way of proving it.

"Silky's right," Jardine decided. "We got to find what's left of the shack and make damn sure Billy's dead."

"Oughta be somethin' — even after three years," opined the hefty George Earl. "Buzzards had to leave somethin'. Maybe a few bones."

"What bones?" scowled Rocklin. "That damn shack was a regular powder-house."

"Too bad we didn't know that," muttered Sturm, "when we threw firebrands."

"No use talking it over," warned Weems. "And no use heading for New Chance unless there's a reasonable doubt Reese escaped before the explosion. So we have to check the site of the old shack and the area surrounding it."

"How long d'you figure . . . ?" began Earl.

"By tomorrow afternoon maybe," said Weems, "if we travel till midnight,

71

make camp and push on again before dawn."

It was 2 p.m. of the next day when the six desperadoes, saddlesore and in ill humor, reached the base of the brush-littered slope deep in the Arido Hills, the scene of their never-to-be-forgotten showdown with their leader.

One by one they dismounted. Bitter memories assailed them as they studied the ruin of the shack, and it spoke volumes for the boss-outlaw's evil influence, the power of his personality, that every man felt for his sidearm. Rocklin grimaced uncomfortably and mouthed a curse.

"What's the matter with us? Crazy sonofabitch has been dead three years."

"Let's not forget the New Chance jail has a guest," said Weems. "And he's no ghost."

They began rummaging in the dust-covered debris, gathering splintered, rotting planks and tossing them clear. Weems lit a cigar and studied the scene through narrowed eyes, assessing details. The shack had been built hard against the base of a hillside. And for what purpose? Obviously prospectors had sheltered in it. But those old fossickers weren't about to make the mistake of storing explosives in their living quarters. More likely they had cached the powder here before venturing forth on another expedition

And how could Reese have survived? He let his mind drift back to those last violent moments before the blast. Scanning the area, he noted the boulders, the clump of timber in which he had deployed his cohorts. They had run Reese to ground here after he deserted them the night before. He recalled now that, when they reached this place, Reese's horse was nowhere in sight. Reese betrayed his position by firing the first shot from the shack's window, creasing Jardine with a rifle-slug.

"Same thing could've happened to the men who built this cabin." He voiced that thought, and his companions paused to frown at him, listening intently. "They planned on making a stand here — if necessary."

"You mean — if they had to hold off an Apache war party?" frowned Sturm.

"Something like that," nodded Weems. "And would they rely on just the plank walls — hoping the raiders wouldn't try to burn them out?"

"Not damn likely," muttered Jardine.

"More likely they kept an ace up their sleeve," opined Weems. "Some kind of escape-hole."

"How about a tunnel?" suggested Earl.

"Oh, hell," breathed Grose, flinching. "I hope we don't find no tunnel."

"I hope we *do*," retorted Rocklin. "That's the only way I'll believe Billy got out."

"And then we'll know for sure," muttered Weems. "He's the man in the New Chance jail."

"If he got out . . . " began Sturm.

"He could've taken the loot with him," finished Earl. "Yeah, he had it all in a sack — and he could've dragged it."

"Check along the base of the hill directly behind the rear foundations," ordered Weems.

Five minutes later, Jardine over-balanced, slumped against the slope and uncovered the opening. The dislodged earth came away and, coughing against the rising dust, Sturm pointed excitedly to the dark hole.

"It's shored!" he whooped. "Look! Timbers at the top and both sides!"

"Ain't much of it," observed Jardine. "No man could walk through it, but . . ."

"It wasn't dug as a regular mine shaft," declared Weems. "All they needed was crawling room. Moving one behind the other, they could travel it all the way to . . ."

"Wherever it ends — yeah." Rocklin nodded eagerly as he retreated to his horse. "Listen, I'll scout around the hillside while one of you tries crawlin' through."

"If Billy got stuck, I'll find his bones in there," grinned Sturm, shrugging out of his jacket. "And maybe the sack!"

"Go carefully," advised Weems.

"Damn tunnel likely caved in years ago," mumbled Grose.

"Not if they braced it all the way," countered Sturm.

Rocklin rode off as Sturm dropped to all fours and crawled into the tunnel entrance. He rejoined the group a short time later, face flushed, eyes a'gleam.

"Don't look for Karl to back out of there," he told them. "He'll get out a little way around the hill. I found the other end of the tunnel. Whole mess o' brush growin' in front of it — but I found it."

Sturm reappeared soon afterward, trudging around the base of the rise with dirt caked on his clothing.

"Found a lamp in there," he reported. "Still enough oil in the tank. I primed the wick and lit her up, checked every

76

foot of the tunnel. That's how Billy gave us the slip, nothin' surer."

"Empty, huh?" prodded Jardine.

"I tell you it's downright weird," muttered Sturm. He was trembling, as he fished out his makings to build a smoke. "Tunnel's shored up, see? But the floor's just bare earth. No way the wind could blow through there these past three years, so I could see . . . "

He paused, wincing uneasily.

"You could see what?" demanded Rocklin.

"He must've crawled through — draggin' the sack behind him," said Sturm. "Drag-marks are still there. And, on one side, just a patch on the floor — I found the clear mark of his hand." He nodded grimly. "Billy's alive all right."

"So the newspapers told it true," frowned Earl. "That's really him in the New Chance lock-up. And — if they hang him before we get there — if he dies without talkin' — we'll *never* see the cash."

77

"Damn near thirty thousand," growled Jardine. "And it's rightly ours."

"The circuit-judge won't reach New Chance before the end of the month — that's what it says in the newspaper," Weems reminded them. "So time is on our side. Today is only the seventh."

"New Chance next stop, huh Silky?" prodded Earl.

"We move west from here," nodded Weems. "Time enough later for planning the break. The important thing is for us to reach New Chance as fast as these horses can carry us. After we arrive, I'll decide how we're gonna separate Reese from the law."

The Mulder buzzard bunch were well and truly on the way to New Chance when the Weems wolf-pack began moving west for the high country.

Pagosa Bend, located 10 miles north of the New Mexico-Colorado border, was the junction closest to New Chance. There the representatives of the big newspaper syndicates arrived by train and stagecoach and compared notes as to how best to travel to their ultimate destination. The Philby coach bound southwest for New Chance couldn't carry the entire party — Freebold of the San Francisco 'Dispatch', McWhirter and Kress, reporter and photographer from the 'Herald', Jennings and Quince of the Chicago 'Tribune', the illustrious Cleaver T. Harmon of the New York 'Observer' and the others, 17 in all.

It was decided they should pool their resources, each man contributing from his expense account, to hire three rigs to transport them to New Chance Pass bag and baggage and in some degree of comfort.

The scribes from the big cities were destined to reach New Chance exactly 30 minutes after the bounty hunters.

4

As Wild As They Claim

WEST of Santa Fe, in the sun-baked plaza of a town called Mendoza, another interested party was learning of the recent events in New Chance. The unpopular character known to Mendoza citizens as Jim Billings was seated by the fountain in the town square, chewing on a cold cigar and staring straight ahead, but eavesdropping on the conversation of two aged locals nearby.

The Mendoza sheriff disliked and distrusted the long-haired, bewhiskered hard case who had haunted the local scene these past few years, and that went double for his deputies and every barkeep in every saloon, every bar-girl, every tablehand, professional gambler, merchant and stablehand. Who could

80

feel drawn to a man so cold-eyed, so hot-tempered, so implacably anti-social? Some called him a prospector. Others assumed him to be nothing better than hermit with uncanny luck at the games of chance. Hermit or not, he was a frequent patron of Mendoza's saloons and, apparently, an inveterate gambler, and no townman approved his attitudes; he had proved himself a sore loser and a gloating, insulting winner. When he lost at poker, the dice or faro, he cursed the dealers. When he won, he derided them.

He changed position slightly, the better to hear the mumbled exchange of the old timers. Under the floppy-brimmed hat, the black hair hung low over his forehead and clear to his shoulders. The eyes glowed from under the dark brows and, thanks to the matted, bushy beard, little more of his face was visible. Was he spare of physique or bulky? Who could say? In Mendoza, he was always attired this way, an outsized duster shrouding him from neck to ankles.

"Uh huh — Bloody Billy for sure," the first old man asserted. "It was all there in the newspaper. They got him stewin' in the calaboose at New Chance. Gonna give him his day in court — end of the month they say — and no jury's about to turn him loose, betcha life on that. So it's a gallows for Billy Reese."

"New Chance — that's way up to the mountains, right?"

"Right. New Chance Pass. Used to be a regular boom town, I hear tell, but all the gold got dug out and now it's real quiet up there I guess."

"Won't be quiet the day they hang Billy."

"Heck, no. He was the meanest, that Billy. There'll be many a man travel many a mile just to make sure that killer gets what's comin' to him."

"Includin' me," reflected the bearded man, rising and slouching across the plaza to the hitch-rail where his horse was tied. "Oh, sure. I ought to be there.

Ain't every man gets to watch himself hang — and attend his own funeral- while he's still alive and kickin'."

Billy Reese, alias Jim Billings, rode west from Mendoza with the intention of stopping by his lonely cabin to pack his saddlebags and bedroll. Curiosity was getting the better of him — curiosity and resentment. Who dared impersonate him, and under these circumstances? What could the masquerader hope to gain? Nothing but a day in court, a brief period of notoriety and then a one-way journey up the wooden steps of a specially-erected gallows.

"This I got to see." He chuckled raspingly as he approached the rim of the basin. "If there's a fool alive with that kind of grief — so much like me that he's gonna hang in my place — I got to see him."

Descending into the basin, his gaze turned toward the site of his cabin, he began cursing bitterly. Two Mendoza lawmen, the sheriff and his chief deputy, were sitting their mounts a few yards from the smoldering timbers. Reese's abode of some three years was a shambles, nought but blackened rubble.

"Must've burned like tinder," the sheriff remarked, when the bearded man reined up beside him. "Bryson and me saw the smoke while we were headed for town along the wagon trail. By the time we got here, the fire had burned itself out."

"Unless you get yourself another place to live, a hotel room maybe," drawled the deputy, "we'll call you a vagrant and invite you to quit the territory."

"You won't be much interested in findin' out who did this," Reese accused the sheriff. "The fire wasn't accidental, and you know it. Bunch of yeller-bellied towners must've worked up the courage to burn me out."

"That'd be my guess," the sheriff calmly declared. "But we didn't see anybody. So what d'you want, Billings? I should interrogate every mother's son in my bailiwick?"

"Somethin' like this had to happen sooner or later," said Bryson. "You're too damn unsociable for your own good, Billings."

"You've never tried to make friends hereabouts," frowned the sheriff. "But, when it comes to making enemies, you got a rare talent. You really work hard at it."

"They've wiped me out," Reese said savagely. "All I got is what's in my pockets and my saddlebags."

"You asking me to believe you had cash stashed here?" challenged the sheriff.

Reese stared morosely at the confusion of charred timbers. Nothing recognizable remained except the heat-twisted frame of a lamp, the blackened skillet, the food-cans that had burst and spewed their contents in the ashes. Every inch of the plank floor had burned, which meant that the balance of his paper cash, some $10,000 secured under a floorboard with adhesive plaster, had gone up in flames.

"How much cash?" demanded Bryson.

"Oh — fifty — maybe sixty dollars," lied Reese. "Well, the hell with it. I'd had all I want of Mendoza anyway."

"So you're quittin'?" prodded the deputy.

"Right here and now," nodded Reese.

"I'm no hypocrite, so I'll say it straight," declared the sheriff. "You won't be missed, Billings. We'll be glad to see the last of you."

"As sure as God made little green apples, that mean streak of yours is gonna be the death of you," predicted Bryson. "And, when you get yours, we'd as soon you're someplace else."

"A long ways from Mendoza County," nodded the sheriff.

"You can quit your whinin'," Reese said derisively. "I'm on my way."

He nudged his mount to movement and, without a backward glance, rode on past the ruin, making for the west slope of the basin.

"Good riddance," muttered the sheriff. "Amen," growled the deputy.

Some 48 hours later, Bloody Billy Reese acquired a packhorse and provisions, also a couple dozen deer-hides in good condition. In New Chance, he would easily unload the skins; merchants were always in the market for such items. The lone trapper, an old timer too weak to defend himself, fell victim to Reese's knife and was buried in a shallow grave. When Reese rode on, nothing remained of the trapper's lonely camp.

★ ★ ★

New Chance was ready for its influx of influential newspapermen and the transformation had Larry and Stretch bewildered; it seemed the half-alive mountain town had changed overnight.

All manner of visitors were arriving by the score. So far reaching was the fame of Bloody Billy that farm-hands and cow-pokes had traveled 100 miles and more from all compass-points. On the suddenly-bustling main street, temporarily inactive cattle-buyers rubbed shoulders with traveling salesmen, prospectors, trappers and representatives of the stagelines and railroads plundered by the Reese gang in its heyday.

And the fair sex was well-represented. A cross-section of frontier matrons and spinsters and ladies of easy virtue, kin or friends of the killer's victims, were here to see justice done. As well as the stage crews and payroll guards, many an ordinary citizen had been cut down by the trigger-happy Billy.

"I'm mighty unpopular, ain't I?"

The man in the second storey cell of the town jail mumbled this remark to the marshal, while staring down through his barred window at the fist-shaking crowd below. Already, people were clamoring for blood.

"Mighty unpopular," said Cyrus, from beyond the celldoor. "But that's no skin off your nose, right? What d'you care if you die unpopular? You'll die famous, Ed — I mean Billy."

"All that matters," shrugged Appleyard, "is the dyin'."

Prices were up. The tariff at the New Chance Hotel, and at all the re-opened rooming houses and doss-joints, had doubled. Informed of this, the Texans had surprised Arnold Shell by calmly surrendering the extra.

"I was counting on putting three, maybe four newspapermen in that double room of yours," he confessed.

"Sorry to disappoint you," drawled Larry. "It just happens we got plenty dinero."

And that was an understatement. The Texans had brought a bankroll of better than $1000 to New Chance; at poker, Larry had been riding a winning streak for the past twelve months.

When they stopped by Mayor Tweedy's emporium to buy tobacco, they found that happy opportunist wearing a broad grin and raising the price of every commodity on his shelves.

From the store they ambled to the Eureka to quench their thirst and pass the time of day with their favorite barkeep. Here, as everywhere else, they were forced to pay more for their pleasure.

"Bonanza for the old town, huh Jake?" remarked Larry, as they worked on their beer. "Nothin' like a trial and a hangin' to boost the population."

"And the prices," growled Stretch.

"I must be gettin' old," complained Jake. "There was Billy Reese — right here in this bar, bellyachin' because some whore double-crossed him and tryin' to blow his lousy brains out — and I didn't recognize him."

"We're all gettin' a mite older," Larry consoled him. "We're all slowin' down."

"Not you two — and especially you," countered Jake. "Hell. The way you jumped him, it happened faster than I could watch." He shook his head dolefully. "I didn't realize who he was till Milo Tweedy started spreadin' the news. And then it hit me. I'd seen that face before on more reward posters than you could count." He changed the subject by confiding, "Jerry Webb got a message from the Pagosa Bend telegrapher. Those big city reporters are arrivin' today."

"Who cares?" Stretch shrugged and grimaced. "You meet one scribbler, you've met 'em all."

"One scribbler you won't mind meetin' is here already," said Jake, grinning knowingly. "Arrived this mornin' and interviewed Reese right-away. He's Russ Newcombe from the Denver Clarion. Rented himself a fast horse in Manassa Gulch."

"You think we'll want to meet him?" frowned Larry.

"I'm damn sure," nodded Jake. "He got a head start on those reporters from Chicago and the west coast, because he don't mind a few saddlesores."

"That don't make him so special," argued Stretch.

"Oh, you'll think so," predicted Jake.

"Why?" demanded Stretch.

"Denver's where he works at his trade," said Jake. "But he was born in Texas." Glancing beyond them, he added, "Get ready to shake his hand. He's headed this way now."

Trading pleased grins, the drifters turned to greet Russ Newcombe. He too was grinning, his hand out-thrust, while their welcoming smiles changed to incredulous frowns.

"Yeah, I know. You can't believe a man so short could be Texan." Slight of build, amiable and good-humored, he stared up at them from his 5 feet, 1 inch. "It's true just the same. I was born and raised in Abbotstown on the San Antonio. Pleasure meeting you, Larry. You too, Stretch." After shaking hands, he nodded to the barkeep. "Refill their glasses, Jake, and join us. And I'll have the same."

"Pleased to meetcha, Russ," said Stretch.

"You're pleased — but still surprised," chuckled Newcombe. "Well, it happens.

I have three brothers working a spread in North Texas — all six-footers. I'm the runt of the litter. Take after my mother, God rest her saintly soul."

"We'll drink to her," Larry suggested.

The publicity-shy adventurers could afford to relax in the company of the derby-hatted little man in the grey striped suit. He made his position clear at once. The Lone Star Hellions were newsworthy at any time but, right now, Billy Reese was the big story.

"That's all I'm here for," he told them. "And that's plenty. So enjoy your booze and drop your guards, gents. Little Russ isn't about to write any far-fetched Larry and Stretch copy."

"Talked to Reese already, have you, Russ?" prodded Jake.

"Made my blood run cold, even with those steel bars between us," confided Newcombe. "I didn't get many answers out of him. He's close-mouthed. Most dangerous-looking hard case I ever laid eyes on."

For 10 minutes or so, during

which time Nils Mulder and his cohorts arrived in New Chance, the expatriates socialized and conversed on their favorite subject, the Lone Star State. Then, with the time close to noon and the Clarion reporter remarking he'd worked up an appetite, the trouble-shooters invited him to be their guest.

"Good chow at the New Chance Hotel," Larry told him, nodding so-long to Jake Sharney. "We'll eat hearty and . . ."

"And keep right on talking about Texas," predicted Newcombe.

"'Less you can think of anything better to talk," grinned Stretch.

The bounty hunters were idling their mounts along the main stem and noting the signs of New Chance's resurgence. Every building, including some never intended as rooming houses, had been taken over by would-be observers of Billy Reese's last moments. The overflow had pitched tents or rigged lean-to's at the edge of town. New

Chance was assuming a festive, feverish look reminiscent of the 4th of July.

Mulder glanced up to the barred window atop Cyrus's office and the barely-visible guest of dishonor.

"There he is, boys," he said softly. "Bloody Billy himself."

"Five thousand bucks' worth of bandido," leered Purvis.

"In Arizona, he will make us rich," muttered Ortega. "In this place — no."

"He won't be in this place after tonight," vowed Mulder.

"We weren't countin' on so big a crowd," frowned Dall.

"That's just a crowd after all," shrugged Mulder. "Rubes and no-accounts here to see the show. They ain't opposition, Dall. So quit your frettin'. 'Tween now and sundown, I'll figure how we're gonna bust Reese out of there."

They were in sight of the New Chance Hotel when Molly Lamont finished trading pleasantries with a passer-by, Jerry Webb the telegrapher, and turned to re-enter the lobby. For a moment, Purvis enjoyed a clear view of her, and that moment was enough.

"I knew this town'd be lucky for me," he grinned, turning his mount toward the hitch-rail. "You see her, Nils? Just my type!"

"Anything in skirts is just your type," shrugged Mulder.

"Here he goes again," jeered Dall.

"You jaspers can get along without me for an hour or two," said Purvis, dismounting hastily. "Tie my horse, Dall. I'm in a hurry."

"We'll stick around a little while," decided Mulder. "I got a feelin' this one can't be sweet-talked, Purvis." He made Dall and the Mexican an offer. "Five bucks says he won't make it to her room."

"I ain't bettin'," said Dall, "on account of I got that same feelin'."

They sat their mounts by the hitch-rail, watching Purvis hustle across the porch to enter the lobby, and paying no attention to the three men crossing the street toward the hotel, one uncommonly short, two uncommonly tall.

As Purvis strode in, Molly emerged from the dining room and started for the passage leading to the kitchen. Her eyebrows rose when the stranger hustled across to bar her way. Flashing his most winning smile, Purvis fished out his come-on bankroll and exhibited it.

"You get the idea, honey? Sure you do. Now what d'you say we get acquainted — *close* acquainted — you know what I mean?"

"You must be mistaking me for somebody else." Molly smiled blandly, but her voice dripped icicles. "Another kind of woman."

"C'mon now, honey," he urged. "Time's a' wastin'."

"You're certainly wasting *my* time," she retorted. "I work here, and it's time for me to help out in the kitchen. Our lunch trade will be coming in and . . ."

"Forget 'em," he leered, grasping her wrist. "What I got in mind is more fun than eatin'. You know what I mean?"

He uttered those words just as the three Texans entered the lobby, and loud enough for at least one of them to hear. Larry kept coming, his jaw jutting aggressively, the knuckles of his right hand tingling in anticipation. Molly, flushed with anger, swung her free hand hard, but the slap won nought but a triumphant chuckle from Purvis, who declared,

"That's fine, honey. I like my women lively."

Staring beyond her assailant, she smiled a greeting.

"You're a welcome sight, Larry. And I'm sure you're hungry. So — if you'll kindly separate me from this Don Juan — I'll help the cook dish up lunch."

"You with the bankroll," growled Larry, tapping Purvis's shoulder. "Stash it back in your pants, let go of the lady — and get the hell out of here."

Molly wrenched free of Purvis as he

turned to scowl at his challenger.

"What's *your* gripe, saddlebum? I'm beatin' your time, huh?"

"Vamoose," ordered Larry.

"Don't try bossin' *me* around!" snapped Purvis, squaring off at him. "I'll leave when I'm good and ready!"

"I've just decided," Larry said coldly. "You're good and ready."

He grasped a fistful of the fancy vest and swung, lifting Purvis off his feet and hurling him all the way to the entrance. And there, while the cursing dude struggled to regain his balance, Stretch helped him on his way, delivering a well-aimed kick to the seat of his pants. Purvis's exit was somewhat less than dignified. He hurtled out to the porch, collided with a post, flopped to the steps and rolled down to the sidewalk, while the Texans emerged, Larry calling a harsh warning.

"And stay away from here!"

Resenting this humiliation of one of his aides, Mulder muttered a command. As Purvis scrambled to his feet, Dall and Ortega dismounted and hurried up to the porch with Mulder in tow; suddenly the bounty hunters were fired with the urge to prove they could not be trifled with. And that proved unwise.

"'Scuse me, little Russ," drawled Stretch.

"Yeah, I know," grinned Newcombe. "You got chores."

Dall, rushing Larry, was checked by a jabbing left and sent backstepping across the porch to collapse on the steps. Stretch moved forward then, blocking the advance of Dall and Ortega, while Larry and Mulder grappled and Purvis maneuvered to strike at Larry from behind. Larry hunched his shoulders and bowed his head when the blow came, and Purvis's fist flashed past to explode in Mulder's face.

The arrival of the big city journalists in three vehicles a few moments later was an anti-climax. In front of the New Chance Hotel where the brawl raged, excited locals and transients jostled for vantagepoints, while the marshal, the mayor, Doc Bayes and other officials strove in vain to restore order.

"Nobody knows we're alive," remarked the dapper Barney Freebold, star reporter of the San Francisco Dispatch.

"First Visit to the wild, wild west — for all of us," said Leo McWhirter of the Herald. "So we'd better get used to the ground rules, Freebold, a brannigan in the main street rates more attention then the arrival of the press."

Joe Kress, McWhirter's traveling companion and the Herald's best photographer, signified agreement with one word.

"Obviously."

Sam Jennings, genial representative of the Chigago Tribune, worked his cigar to the side of his mouth and good-humoredly observed,

"The two tall guys look like they could take on the whole town — and win."

His sidekick muttered a comment, and fervently. Hubert Quince, young and reticent with sensitive features, was the only press-artist in the group. The Tribune's editor had been known to brag that the on-the-scene sketches of Hubert Quince were more graphic, more personal than any photograph.

"It's a revelation," declared Quince. "There's a certain poetic rhythm — something artistic — in the way those tall men fight."

"Just another brawl," opined Cleaver T. Harmon, celebrated feature writer of the New York Observer.

The end came abruptly, and Quince was profoundly impressed. For the fourth time in that slugging match, Larry scored a blow that sent Purvis reeling. And Mulder, rising groggily beside a water trough, was too dazed to move clear. He went over backward after Purvis collided with him, flopping into the trough. Stretch, meanwhile, was discouraging Dall and Ortega, maintaining a merciless grip on their collars and batting their heads together.

"Now see here, gents!" Tweedy bellowed to the Texans. "This has gone far enough!" He gestured to the stalled vehicles. "What're our guests gonna think of New Chance? All this rowdy hell-raisin' — it's apt to give our town a bad name!"

"They're all though anyway," shrugged Stretch, releasing his would-be attackers so that they crumpled to the dust.

"Marshal . . . !" began Tweedy.

"No need to — uh — make a case out of it," called Mulver. He struggled from the trough shedding water and shivering, but fast regaining his presence of mind. Taking a warning grip on Purvis's arm, he assured Tweedy and Cyrus. "It was just a little misunderstandin'. Nothin' serious. And — uh — we applogize for the disturbance."

"I got my hands full — guardin' an *important* prisoner," Cyrus declared for the benefit of the visiting journalists. "Else I'd throw you trouble-makers in my calaboose."

"Calaboose — you ever hear such a word?" Jennings dryly commented to

Freebold. "Western terminology. Why don't they call it a jail and be done with it?"

At Mulder's urging, Dall, Ortega and Purvis untied their horses and led them away. Tweedy then delivered his speech of welcome and the locals made way for the scribes descending from the rented rigs. They were conducted into the hotel by Arnold Shell and his wife, the mayor and his cronies crowding in to introduce themselves, volunteers following with the baggage.

In the lobby, Newcombe lost track of Larry and Stretch, who had gone on into the dining room; nothing like a wild brawl to put an edge on their appetites. The runty representative of the Denver Clarion was enjoying the experience of hob-nobbing with his more illustrious colleagues. At first, Jennings, Freebold and Company were inclined to write him off as a small-time frontier journalist. But he quickly corrected that impression by confiding, "I arrived a mite earlier than you gents. Matter of fact I've already interviewed Reese and wired a report to my editor."

"My compliments, Newcombe," said Jennings, pumping his hand. "Got to say you work fast."

"Well . . . " Newcombe shrugged modestly. "We don't let the grass grow under our feet — not when we're onto a story so big."

"Is he as tough as they claim?" demanded Freebold.

"Seven counts of murder?" frowned Harmon.

"Wait till you meet this jasper," said Newcombe. "He's a mean one, I'm telling you. And those seven murders — don't forget those were only his *known* victims."

A short distance west of town, temporarily camped, the bounty hunters discussed their next move. Mulder, squatting on a rock with steam rising from his sodden clothing, dismissed the brawl as being of no consequence.

"Our business in this burg is more

important than tanglin' with a couple saddletramps." Scowling at the bedraggled Purvis, he added, "And more important than chasin' women."

"We could maybe make our move tonight," suggested Dall.

"Tomorrow," countered Mulder. "Just before sun-up — when the marshal and the whole town'll only be half-awake."

5

A Little Local Color

THE city men enjoyed that lunch, their first meal in New Chance, maybe more than they had anticipated. Sam Jennings complimented Shell on his cuisine and expressed satisfaction with the accommodation provided. Not so Cleaver T. Harmon, who bitterly objected to sharing a room with the loudly-talkative Oscar Bennet, assistant editor of the Dayton Chronicle. Shell apologized to the New York journalist while the other newsmen ate hungrily, watched by Larry and Stretch from their corner table.

"Scribblers — they're all the same," mused Stretch, forking up a mouthful of chicken. "Big-talkin' busybodies. 'Cept Russ, of course. Bein' Texan, he's got more savvy."

"At least they ain't plaguin' *us*," Larry pointed out. "So we might's well stay on. For as long as Russ is here anyway."

Stretch munched and swallowed and observed,

"There's another feller takin' a shine to Molly. But, this time, she ain't objectin'."

"Girl as pretty as her," shrugged Larry. "Only natural some buck'd admire her."

"He just talked to her," Stretch reported. "And she talked back at him, smilin' real friendly, so I guess he's actin' respectful."

"That way he stays out of trouble," said Larry.

"He's quit eatin'." Stretch was becomingly becoming keenly interested in the unassuming Hubert Quince. "Now he's writin' on the bill of fare — and he keeps starin' at her. Hey. You suppose he's writin' a love-letter already?"

Larry followed Quince's movements a moment and made an accurate guess. Molly was being kept busy, moving from table to table, gathering used dishes and exchanging remarks with the out-of-towners, and it seemed Quince's pencil kept working even while his eyes were on her.

"That hombre ain't writin'. I think he's makin' a picture of her. A sketch, you know?"

When Molly next passed by the table at which Quince sat, he spoke to her again, presented the quick portrait and mumbled a few words. She blushed prettily, patted at her hair and murmured a rejoinder. And then, eager to show off, she came to the corner table.

"Larry, Stretch, look! That gentle-talking Mister Quince is an artist. Drew a picture of me."

They studied Quince's handiwork with the awe of outdoors men unacquainted with the creative arts. To them, it seemed the press artist had

109

worked a miracle. A striking likeness of Molly Lamont had been achieved deftly and with economy of line. Everything that mattered was there, including the set of her pretty head and the dimples, the characteristic tilt of her well-shaped chin.

"And he signed it, see?" she enthused. "And — oh my! He's such a gentleman." Retrieving the sketch, she frowned pensively and wondered, "What must he think of us — and New Chance? I mean, a young man so refined and artistic. He seems terribly nervous, and who could blame him?"

"You frettin' about him?" challenged Larry.

She blushed again and said defensively, "They're our guests after all. Up to us to — well — to make them feel at home."

"Well, sure," he nodded. "But there's only so much you can do, Molly. You can't change New Chance."

"And New Chance ain't nothin' like Chicago," opined Stretch.

"Could I ask you something?" she pleaded. "You're good at what you do. Like, for instance, the way you whipped that dirty-mouthed dude and his good-for-nothing friends — and you without a bruise to show for it."

"So?" prodded Larry.

"So do me a favor," she said softly. "If you should see Mister Quince in — well — a difficult situation . . . "

"Howzat again?" frowned Stretch.

"You know," said Molly. "Some roughneck crowding him or a barkeep trying to get him drunk or somebody picking his pocket. You'd take care of him, wouldn't you? Just to please me?"

"We'll take care of any galoots that gang up on your gentleman friend," Larry gravely promised. "Just to please you."

"And us," grinned Stretch.

Right after lunch, the visiting journalists were rounded up by the town council and taken on a short tour of New Chance and environs, with special emphasis on the abandoned diggings, the Tweedy Emporium, the Eureka Saloon and the gallows under construction in Bonanza Road, all this in the interests of offering the newsmen a little local color. Predictably, they took notes. Joe Kress set up his camera and took a few pictures and Hubert Quince made sketches.

The visitors were then formally presented to Cyrus Hindmarsh and, mindful of the mayor's instructions, the marshal answered their questions tersely, striving to present the stern, leather-tough image of what the guests assumed to be a typical frontier lawman.

"A man of few words, the marshal," remarked Jennings, as they followed Tweedy upstairs.

"Taciturn would be putting it mild," grinned Freebold.

"Mildly," corrected Harmon.

"That's what gripes me about feature writers," jeered Freebold. "They're over-educated."

"And now, gentlemen, the moment you've been waitin' for," the mayor said proudly, conducting them to the occupied cell. "Here he is — the one and only Bloody Billy Reese — the West's most cold-blooded killer. Stand up, Reese!"

Well-rehearsed and savoring his new-found notoriety, Appleyard came upright and stood grinning insolently at the city men. They fired their questions, all of which he blocked with the retort,

"I'll save my braggin' till the trial."

"Proud of what you've done, are you, Billy?" challenged Jennings, scribbling furiously.

"You ever kill a woman, Billy?" asked Freebold.

"I ain't sayin'," growled Appleyard.

"How am I gonna get my damn-blasted camera set up-with all those bars between him and me?" demanded Kress.

"No problem for me," muttered Quince, his pencil busy. "I'll include the bars in my picture. Good atmosphere."

"What got you started on the outlaw trail, Billy?" asked Bennett.

"Who did you hate most?" Harmon gravely enquired. "Your father or your mother?"

"Aw, for cryin' out loud, Cleave!" gibed McWhirter. "You and your psychological mumbo jumbo!"

"Your readers, being low-brows, will settle for gory details," Harmon said loftily. "I'm thankful to say my copy is aimed at a more literate, intellectual public."

"He's got his own private office in New York," McWhirter remarked to Freebold.

"Doilies on his desk, I bet," grinned Freebold.

"What I want to know is how'd Bloody Billy get caught so easily?" Jennings eyed the prisoner expectantly. "Slowing down? Conscience getting at you, Billy? You seeing ghosts — all the people you've killed?"

"I ain't sayin' nothin' else." Appleyard suddenly showed spirit, startling Tweedy

114

and Cyrus by ad-libbing. "Hey, Marshal! Get these slickers outa here — 'fore I lose my temper!"

"The hell with him," shrugged Freebold. "Let's go."

"Okay by me," grunted Jennings. "You finished your sketch, Quince?"

"Finished," said Quince.

"Bet you'd rather work on something prettier, huh?" Jennings winked at his colleagues. "Like that good-looking waitress at the hotel?"

"She's not just a waitress, Sam," frowned Quince. "She's the hotelkeeper's niece — and a lady."

"Did I say she isn't a lady?" challenged Jennings. "Listen, young feller, maybe she's the first girl you ever fell for, but you don't have to be so damn sensitive about it."

"Artistic temperament," gibed McWhirter. "You agree, Professor Harmon?"

Ignoring McWhirter, the New Yorker appealed to Tweedy.

"How can I get background material on this butcher? My readers will expect something more significant than a list of his victims. And, if he won't talk . . . "

"I'm glad you reminded me, Mister Harmon," beamed Tweedy. "Darn near forgot to offer you gents the full co-operation of our own newspaper office. The Gazette holds a fat file on Billy, and Doc Bayes knows every line of every report by heart."

"Bayes — oh, sure," nodded Freebold. "He broke the story right here in New Chance. The Gazette was the first paper to — hey! Did you call him Doc?"

"If he's a qualified physician . . . " began Harmon.

"Well and truly," Cyrus assured him.

"And the best Doc in the whole northwest area," declared Tweedy.

"A croaker running a newspaper," frowned Jennings, making a note. "Now that's a switch. Ought to be worth a couple paragraphs."

"So what're we waiting for?" Bennett asked impatiently. "Let's go talk to him."

"I'll need to consult him anyway," muttered Harmon, as they retreated to the stairs. "My sinus condition has worsened since I left New York."

Until late afternoon, Doc Bayes played host to the big city journalists, enjoying their company, their sardonic humor. He put the files at their disposal, allowed himself to be cajoled into a 20-minute speech on the subject of frontier medical practice and answered their questions as best he could. And, grudgingly impressed by his first report of the Reese arrest — described by Freebold as 'graphic' and 'imaginative' — the city men accorded him due respect; there were no patronizing remarks. The only disappointed scribe was Cleaver T. Harmon, whose sinus condition Doc described as mild — also incurable.

Larry and Stretch, meanwhile, were learning something of Billy Reese's character from the head bartender at the Eureka. Jake Sharney had carried a badge during the years of Reese's outlawry, had talked with several of his victims — a maimed stagecoach guard, a permanently-disfigured bank cashier, an exdeputy sheriff confined to a wheelchair and, most informative of all, a member of the old Reese gang wounded during a bank hold-up and abandoned by his old boss.

"Because that poor dumb thief — feller name of Hibbs — was wounded too bad to mount his horse," Jake confided, "Reese put a bullet in him before he led the rest of the outfit away. Didn't want Hibbs taken alive — and interrogated."

"Runt, you did wrong," opined Stretch, gulping his whiskey. "You should've let that skunk shoot himself."

"Well, this Hibbs feller cashed in, but not rightaway," muttered Jake. "He talked. Oh, sure. Had plenty to say about the famous Billy Reese."

"Bad medicine, huh?" prodded Larry.

"I've known all kinds of outlaws," declared Jake. "Some of 'em — even

118

a killer or two — I could damn near respect. But not Reese. Listen, you and Stretch have been around and seen a lot, known many killer, so you got to agree with me. The worst kind, the most low-down of all, is the kind who *enjoys* it."

"No argument," growled Larry.

"That's how Reese is," Jake assured them. "No matter how he kills, with a gun, a knife or his bare hands, he likes to make 'em suffer. Hibbs told me Reese'd laugh like crazy for an hour or more after he'd butchered some poor galoot." He left them long enough to attend his other customers. Rejoining them, he poured refills and offered his opinion regarding the forthcoming trial. "The law will treat him fair. They're bringin' in a Santa Fe lawyer to defend him and, between now and then, Cy Hindmarsh'll have his nose in a mess of law books on account of he has to be prosecutor. Well, Cy ain't the smartest marshal I ever knew, and he's no lawyer, but you can still bet on Reese hangin'. Ain't a jury in the whole country would acquit him, nor a judge that wouldn't deliver a death sentence."

Later that evening, when the reporters gathered at the Eureka, the Texans were singled out by Hubert Quince. Diffident and choosing his words with care, the press artist introduced himself, recalled they seemed closely acquainted with Miss Molly Lamont and hopefully enquired,

"Do you happen to know if the young lady is — uh — engaged to be married? Does she have a suitor?"

"Fancy free, far as we know," shrugged Larry. "We've only been here a few days."

"But she's a friend of ours," offered Stretch. "I reckon, if she had a beau, she'd of mentioned him."

"That's very gratifying, and I hope you'll excuse my asking such a personal question about her," said Quince, "but I assure you it's not idle curiosity on my part."

"I think what Hubert means," Stretch remarked to Larry, "is he's took a shine to Molly."

"I think that's what he means," nodded Larry.

"You don't object?" prodded Quince.

"Ain't up to us, amigo," drawled Larry. "We ain't kin to her. Friends, sure. But just passin' through."

"Please believe," Quince said solemnly, "my intentions are honorable."

"I should hope," frowned Stretch.

"All the luck, Hubert," offered Larry. "That's as much as we can say. Can't offer any advice about how to court her. We wouldn't know how."

"On account of," explained Stretch, "we're kinda womanshy. What I mean, we get along fine with females, but we're leery of weddin' bells, you know?"

"Confirmed bachelors," nodded Quince. "I too was a confirmed bachelor — until my first glimpse of Miss Lamont." He sipped his beer

121

reflectively. "I'm sure she'd be happy in Chicago."

"I hear tell that's a lively burg," said Larry.

"I live in the quietest part, the Langworth section," said Quince. "Yes, I know I could make her happy, and she's wasted in a town like New Chance. If only I could work up the courage to ask her . . . "

"When that time comes, you'll be on your own," pointed out. "Some things a man just has to do for himself."

"You've been patient, and I appreciate it," said Quince. "May I repay your kindness by offering a little advice?"

"If you think we need it," grinned Larry.

Quince glanced warily to the side table where his traveling companion, Sam Jennings, good-humoredly conversed with Freebold, McWhirter and Bennett.

"Sam's trying to organize a game," he confided. "Poker. Those other reporters are from San Francisco and

Dayton, Ohio, so they don't know his reputation. I think he's looking for an extra player."

"And . . . ?" demanded Larry.

"For the sake of your bankroll, and no matter how much you enjoy poker, don't get involved," advised Quince. "Please, don't misunderstand. It's not that Sam cheats. It's just he's the champion poker player of the whole Chicago press."

At that, Larry's eyes gleamed. Stretch shrugged resignedly and assured Quince,

"You ain't warnin' Larry at all. You're *invitin'* him."

"Fifty," said Larry. "You got my word, big feller. That's all I'll take into the game."

"Your word's good enough for me," said Stretch. "But — uh . . . " He held out a hand, "I'll hold our dinero, all but the fifty, in case you get to feelin' rash."

Larry surrendered all but $50 of their combined bankroll and ambled across to join the journalists. As he pulled up a chair, Jennings grinned at him and remarked,

"This might get too rich for your blood, cowboy. I saw you and your buddy in a donnybrook and doing just fine. But poker is a different kind of fight."

"Don't worry about me," shrugged Larry. "I'm no sore loser."

"Well — we'll damn soon find out," chuckled Jennings. He tore the wrapper of a new deck and set it down. "Cut for deal."

At midnight, when the game broke up, Larry pocketed his winnings, paid for a last round of drinks and bade the reporters so-long. He ambled out of the Eureka with his original stake plus $100, most of which had come from the Jennings bankroll. Stretch rose from a caneback on the saloon porch, yawned boredly and asked,

"How'd we make out?"

"That Jennings better be one helluva newspaperman," said Larry, as they sauntered to the hotel. "That's the only way he'll keep eatin'."

"Pushover, huh?" prodded Stretch.

"If he's the best of the Chicago newspaper crowd, I'd enjoy to tangle with the worst of 'em," drawled Larry.

"He contributed to our bankroll?" asked Stretch.

"Near a hundred dollars' worth," nodded Larry.

"Every little helps," said Stretch.

From behind his bar, Jake Sharney grinned scathingly at the newsmen. Quince was slumped in a chair near the poker table, thoughtfully leafing through his sketch-pad; he had drawn quick portraits of the players during that memorable game. McWhirter was anxiously checking the deck, inspecting every card. Freebold and Bennett were gloomily tallying their cash and Jennings was pouring himself a much-needed booster.

"Deck's clean," reported McWhirter. "Not one card marked."

"I swear that Kentucky cowhand must've learned the game before his

125

voice broke," muttered Freebold.

"That last hand," recalled Bennett. "Damn his nerve, he bluffed us with a pair of lousy fives."

"You're the big loser, Jennings," said Freebold. "So how do *you* feel?"

"Fatalistic," lied Jennings. "First thing that Tennessee guy told us was he's no sore loser. Well, that goes for me too. If you can't take your losses with a smile . . ."

"You aren't smiling," observed Freebold.

"And he's not from Tennessee — nor Kentucky. He's a Texan," said Quince.

"Who cares?" scowled Jennings. "One southern drawl sounds the same as another."

"I've had enough for one night," announced Freebold, rising. "You coming, Jennings?"

"In a little while," said Jennings. "So-long, boys. See you at breakfast." He watched the two 'Frisco reporters dawdle out, followed by the Ohio man. Then, turning to Quince, he mumbled

126

a plea. "As a personal favor, Quince, don't let on to the other Chicago men. And not a word about this when we get home. Look, I don't mind losing — just this once — but if all those wise guys in the Criminal Court building ever learned I'd been outsmarted by a rube Texas saddletramp . . . "

"Could we come to terms?" asked Quince. "I'll keep my mouth shut, Sam . . . "

"If . . . ?" challenged Jennings.

"If you'll stop ribbing me about Molly Lamont," said Quince. "It's no laughing matter, Sam. I'm serious about her."

"Don't lose much time, do you?" grinned Jennings. "All right, Rembrandt, it's a deal."

"One other point," said Quince, later, while they were walking to the hotel. "I've talked a little with Larry Valentine . . . "

"And sketched him," nodded Jennings. "Yeah, I know what you're gonna say, buddy. You can learn a lot about a man by drawing a picture of him."

"Well, I wouldn't dismiss him as just another rube, if I were you," advised Quince.

"When it comes to poker, I got to admit he's smarter than he looks," said Jennings. "And he's good with his fists. So what does that make him? Some kind of genius?"

"I don't claim he's a genius," Quince said cautiously. "But, if I were a gambler, I'd bet my last dollar he's more than just a shiftless saddletramp. A special kind of westerner. Experienced. Resourceful. Quick-witted."

"All I'm gonna remember about him," sighed Jennings, "is the way he plays poker."

By 1.30 a.m., New Chance was tomb-quiet, its last light extinguished.

A few minutes before dawn, Arnold Shell came wide awake for the fifth time since retiring. He was as elated as his fellow-councilmen at the prospect of New Chance's second boom, also over-awed by the audacity of their wild scheme. There had to be a side effect of this nervous excitement. Milo Tweedy's digestion was giving him hell. Roscoe Lippert was becoming a brandy-addict, Cyrus Hindmarsh was smoking too much and, in Shell's case, the side effect was insomnia; he hadn't enjoyed a full night's sleep since the arrest of Ed Appleyard, alias Billy Reese.

Slowly and quietly, loath to disturb his slumbering spouse, he slid from their bed and moved to the table by the window. He glanced along the silent street while fumbling for a cigar and, as his gaze fastened on the area fronting the jail-house, his heart seemed to skip a beat.

Something amiss down there. Three shadowy figures moving up to the law office porch. A lynch party? Or some of Reese's old accomplices here to liberate him? Damn and blast!

To whom could he turn in this moment of crisis? To summon Milo, Oley, Roscoe and Jerry would be worse than useless; in a confrontation with armed and desperate outlaws they would be out of their element. On a sudden inspiration, he donned robe and slippers and crept from the room. Those Texans, Valentine and Emerson, were men of some reputation.

"Supposed to be trouble-shooters — if I can believe those wild stories Nick Fleischer used to print. Fast with their guns and their wits. Well, maybe they'll know how to handle this."

The Texans roused to the urgent rapping on their door. While Larry fumbled for his matches, Stretch padded across to open the door. Shell entered quickly, undeterred by the cocked .45 in the taller Texan's fist.

"Don't light the lamp, Valentine! Listen — this is — I mean it could be — a matter of life and death!"

He said his piece while they pulled on pants and boots and buckled their gunbelts, and then they were quitting the room, neither of them pausing to question him; he had said all they needed to hear.

Since the arrest, Cyrus Hindmarsh had slept on the couch in his office. He came to his senses sluggishly, grimacing from the taste in his mouth, resenting this early summons. Before unlocking the street-door, he asked,

"Who?"

"Nelson's the name," muttered Mulder, his face pressed to the panels. "From the U.S. marshal's office. Open up. This is important!"

"Well, I should hope," mumbled Cyrus.

He turned the key, pulled the door open, then retreated with Mulder's cocked six-gun prodding his chest and his eyes dilating in shock. Dall moved in after him with Purvis following, the latter pausing to re-secure the door. At bewildering speed, the marshal was hogtied and gagged and tossed back onto the couch. Purvis stood over him while Mulder and Dall, toting the lawman's keying, hustled up the stairs.

Appleyard rose from his bunk, blinking perplexedly, as the bounty hunters unlocked the cell-door.

"Not one word outa you," warned Mulder. "We're gonna do this quiet, savvy? You try hollerin', we'll gunwhip you and tie you over a horse. Rather travel astride, wouldn't you? Right! Move out!"

During this action, Larry and Stretch had crossed Main Street a block uptown from the hotel. They were moving along the north alley now, headed for the rear of the jailhouse and Bonanza Road. Larry, as usual, was playing a hunch. No sign of the marauders' horses. And where better to hide them than around the corner?

"Shell claims he saw three," muttered Stretch. "But there'd have to be one more at least, huh? Guardin' their horses?"

"You take care of him," ordered Larry. "Work fast, and maybe you'll

132

have time to lend a hand with the others."

"Where'll you be?" demanded Stretch.

"On the porch," grinned Larry. "Right beside of that front door."

6

'He Knows Me!'

BY the time Larry reached the street end of the side alley and climbed up to the law office porch, Stretch was entering Bonanza Road and advancing on the Mexican guarding the four horses. Ortega was at the Main Street corner, all his attention focussed on the jailhouse, when the taller Texan loomed behind him and swung his righthand Colt, denting his sombrero, raising a lump on his cranium and knocking him senseless.

As silently as a marauding Comanche, he hurried along to the law office porch. Larry, clearly visible in the first light of dawn, pantomined instructions from his position left of the street-door. Nodding agreement, Stretch holstered his weapon and hunkered behind the rocking chair right of the door. His partner's gestured warning was explicit. No gunplay at the start.

In the office, Mulder grinned triumphantly at his cohorts. He was grasping Appleyard by his shirt-collar, after gagging him and tying his hands behind his back. Over by Cyrus's desk, sampling his whiskey, Purvis leered back at the boss hunter and remarked,

"Easy pickin's."

"Even so, we'll take no chances," decided Mulder. "Dall, you go on out and make sure nobody's watchin'. We'll come when you give us the word."

Dall made the Texans' chore easier by stepping out and closing the door behind him. He glanced toward the rocker, then froze to the feel of a gun-muzzle prodding his neck.

"Call 'em out," whispered Larry, "or you're grave-bait!"

"How about it?" demanded Mulder.

With sweat beading on his brow, Dall called,

"All — clear . . ."

Larry promptly clobbered him with the Colt's barrel, heaved him over the side-rail and into the alley and was resuming his position beside the door as Purvis turned the knob. The dude moved out, followed by Appleyard propelled by Mulder and, for the next few seconds, confusion reigned. Mulder was grasped from behind by Stretch, lifted and hurled into the street. He struck the sidewalk with a resounding thud and an irate yell, while Purvis whirled to gape incredulously at Larry, who was buffeting Appleyard back into the office and closing the door. The dude mouthed an oath, dropped his right hand and was still pawing for his Colt when Stretch bounded across the porch, swinging. Dazed by that glancing blow, Purvis spun off-balance and toppled down the steps. Mulder jerked him to his feet and, drawing their weapons, they started for the corner of Main and Bonanza at a stumbling run.

The first two shots jerked every newsman in the hotel wide awake, not to mention the other guests and two-thirds of the townfolk.

"I've been expecting this," Jennings said bitterly, as he struggled into his pants. Quince rose from the other bed, blinking uneasily, as he added, "Sooner or later, some galoot'd have to cut loose with a six-gun. Local color, you know?"

"Well . . . " began Quince, on his way to the window.

"Tradition of the wild west," jeered Jennings. "They're staging a shoot-up — for our benefit. I tell you these local hicks are publicity-hungry. Next — mark my words — some idiot will stampede a herd of cattle along the main street."

In the next room, McWhirter and Kress were endangering their lives, leaning so far out their window they almost lost balance.

"It's a gunfight!" gasped Kress. "Hey, Leo! Help me with my camera!"

"It's a set-up!" bellowed Jennings.

"It's no set-up!" yelled Freebold from the third window along. "One of those guys is leaking genuine blood!"

By the time the reporters spilled out onto the hotel porch half-dressed, Mulder and Purvis had reached the corner. Ortega had revived and was dashing to their aid, triggering fast at the Texans on the porch, and Purvis, without Mulder's arm to support him, was slumping to the sidewalk, his gun dropping from his bloodied hand.

"Duck!" cried McWhirter.

The newsmen collapsed in disorder as a ricocheting slug gouged a chunk from a porch-post. From their prone positions, they witnessed the last exchange of shots, Mulder sprawling from the impact of a bullet grazing his right leg, Ortega yelping, throwing his pistol away and raising his hands, demoralized by a Texas bullet searing his left ear.

While the reporters, the town council and some two dozen locals and transients began hurrying to the jailhouse, Larry and Stretch calmly ejected their spent shells and reloaded. Stretch then moved into the side alley to retrieve Dall, who was groggily coming to his senses.

At Tweedy's insistence, the reporters held back. Entering the office, the mayor stared aghast at lawman and prisoner, Cyrus still huddled on the couch, helpless, Appleyard squatting on the floor, mumbling through his gag. Slamming and locking the door, Tweedy advanced on Cyrus.

"Not a word!" he gasped, as he began untying him. "Take this galoot back to his cell and — for pity's sake — leave all the talkin' to me! I'll figure some way of satisfyin' those reporters!"

"They got the drop on me," groaned Cyrus, relieved of his gag. "I dunno if they were gonna lynch him or what. All I know is they busted in here and . . . "

"Shuddup!" ordered Tweedy. "Give me time to *think*!"

Outside, watched by the bug-eyed reporters, the Texans were ascertaining the identity of their victims. Stretch coaxed prompt answers from Dall in his own time-saving fashion, cocking one of his Colts and pressing the muzzle against Dall's throbbing head.

"No, we didn't come to see him free!" wailed Dall.

"Funny," grunted Larry. "That's exactly how it looked."

"I mean — we were just transferrin' him — kind of," explained Dall. "Across the border and into Arizona. There's no bounty on him in New Chance. If we could've delivered him to Pennant Butte, we'd collect five thousand."

"Bounty hunters," sneered Stretch.

"How'd they reach Reese?" demanded Jennings. "They kill the marshal?"

"Well, I saw three of them on the porch when I looked out my window," offered Shell. "And then — fearing the worst — I appealed to Valentine and Emerson to . . . ."

"Cyrus is gonna be just fine!" announced Tweedy, emerging from the office. "But it took all three of 'em to overpower him — and we've learned a harsh lesson from this — uh — wanton and lawless attempt to free Reese. From now on, our marshal will have special guards to assist him twenty-four hours a day. I'll depute 'em before breakfast."

"How does Reese feel?" asked Freebold.

"What's Billy got to say about all this?" challenged McWhirter. "But for McEntire and Henderson, he'd be on his way to Arizona by now."

"Valentine and Emerson," corrected Quince. "You ought to use their right names. After all, they risked their lives to prevent a jailbreak."

"Let me through, damnitall!" panted Doc Bayes, struggling to force his way through the growing crowd.

"Stand aside for Editor Bayes,"

grinned Bennett.

"*Doc* Bayes," insisted Doc, "if anybody's bleeding."

"That's us!" cried Purvis. "Me and Mulder! We're gonna die for sure — unless we're doctored fast!"

The bedraggled dude lurched toward the law office porch with Mulder limping after him and Ortega bringing up the rear. Cyrus emerged from the office then, fully dressed and hefting his shotgun, assuming a stern expression for the benefit of the reporters. He was grimly announcing the prisoner had been returned to his cell, when Freebold called a challenge to Larry.

"Hey, Valentine, these jokers look familiar to you?"

"Same bunch you tangled with yesterday," complained Tweedy. "Plague take 'em! Is our town gonna be over-run by riff-raff — at the greatest era in its history?"

"I'm bleedin' to death!" groaned Mulder. "While you're makin' a speech!"

"You'll live," scowled Doc, after a cursory inspection of his creased ribs. He made a hasty check of Purvis's wound, a shallow bullet-gash along his right forearm, then ordered his patients into the law office. "I'll patch 'em," he told Tweedy. "And then you can do what you like with 'em."

"Inside," ordered Stretch, gesturing with his Colt.

The four bounty hunters trudged into the office to have their wounds tended under Cyrus's supervision. Questioned by the journalists, Tweedy angrily assured them Mulder and his pals would be held for the circuit-judge on charges of attempted kidnapping, assault on an officer of the law, etc, etc, etc.

This tirade was interrupted by Cyrus, who came to the door-way to growl a reminder.

"That'd make five prisoners in all, Mister Mayor. An extra four that have to be fed at the council's expense — and guarded day and night."

"Marshal Hindmarsh, if you got any better ideas . . . " began Tweedy.

"They're bounty-hunters — scavengers — no-accounts," said Cyrus. "We should run 'em out of town. Doc says they'll be fit to ride. And, after this ruckus, they ain't liable to come sneakin' back again."

"Cy's got a point, Milo," opined Shell.

"Get rid of 'em," urged Lippert.

"We got Billy," Craydon pointed out. "What do we need with a bunch of bounty-hunters?"

"Well, I'll go along with the majority decision," said Tweedy. "Our marshal and his special deputies can — uh — concentrate all their efforts on the *big* chore — if they only got the one prisoner."

"Frontier justice is flexible, huh Jennings?" grinned McWhirter.

"Flexible is certainly the word," agreed Jennings.

"But, in a rough and ready way, there's logic in their reasoning,"

144

remarked Quince. "It's a small town jail after all. Not a city lock-up with a staff of armed police and guards. They just don't have the facilities for coping with . . . "

"Sure, sure," nodded Jennings. "A big-shot like Billy Reese is as much responsibility as they can handle."

"All right, folks!" Tweedy called to the crowd. "Let's break it up now, huh? Excitement's over. Gettin' near time for breakfast."

Russ Newcombe grinned and winked at Larry and Stretch before starting back to the hotel with McWhirter and the other newsmen.

"Just like yesterday," mused McWhirter. "Two against four. Fists yesterday. Guns today. Couple real warriors, those buddies of yours."

"Why, sure." Newcombe gestured airily. "Easy chore for Larry and Stretch."

"But they were outnumbered both times," Freebold pointed out.

"With them, winning is kind of a

habit," drawled Newcombe.

After breakfast, Jerry Webb was kept busy. The telegraph office became a hive of activity, journalists crowding in to compose or dictate their version of the breakout attempt to their editors. Sore and sorry, Nils Mulder and his cronies were escorted to the western outlet of New Chance Pass and invited to make themselves scarce — or else. Doc Bayes returned to the Gazette office. Tweedy, Shell and Lippert set about recruiting special guards to assist Cyrus, and Larry and Stretch took their ease in the barroom of the Eureka, socializing with Jake Sharney and Russ Newcombe. The day had begun violently, but now they were relaxed, certain they had seen the last of the bounty-hunters.

Toward noon, more busybodies arrived, an itinerant preacher determined to save the immortal soul of Billy Reese, three tinhorns in a surrey, on the lookout for fresh pickings among

New Chance's growing population of opportunists, two wagon-loads of theatrical folk, the Walter Pearey Traveling Show, seeking a barn or hall in which to stage '3 Hours Of Non-Stop Music And Mirth' — exotic dances, frontier ballads and a one-act play specially written by Pearey himself, 'The Hangman Came At Dawn'.

The cult of tents and lean-to's west of town was spreading fast; soon New Chance's shanty area would be double the size of its business sector. Business was brisk in every saloon. Peddlers hawked their wares along Main Street to the disgust of Milo Tweedy who had no cause to complain; his store was doing a roaring trade.

★ ★ ★

At sundown, Silky Weems and his cohorts finished the long ascent from the east and entered New Chance. Two abreast, Weems and Rocklin leading,

147

they moved slowly along the brightly lit main street. This was more than they had expected — the town teaming with life, a clamor of laughter from every saloon, the hotels and rooming houses filled to capacity and, seated on the porch of the marshal's office, two hefty volunteers nursing shotguns and studying all newcomers intently.

Weems didn't give vent to his chagrin until they were dismounting in front of a livery stable.

"Damn these ghouls," he breathed. "They've been arriving by the score. I thought we'd get here before . . . "

"We're late," Rocklin said flatly. "I'd say about three days late."

"This is gonna make it one helluva dangerous chore," opined Jardine. "Grabbin' Billy — in a town so crowded. Hell! It's like they had another gold-strike!"

The stablehand appeared in the barn entrance, calling to them.

"No vacancies, gents. You might's well move on to the edge of town.

That's where most of our visitors are camped."

Weems shrugged impatiently, turning back toward his horse so quickly that he collided with a passer-by. The little man, Russ Newcombe, regained his balance and began an apology.

"Pardon, friend. Guess I'm getting clumsy . . . "

His voice choked off. They were close enough to a street-lamp for him to clearly see Weems' face, and vice versa. A nerve twitched at Weems' temple as, wide-eyed and apprehensive, the journalist dashed away. Weems darted a glance behind him. The stablehand had retreated into the barn.

"What the hell . . . ?" began Rocklin.

"He knows me!" gasped Weems. "He recognized me — and I'll be gallows-bait if he reaches the local law. Get after him, Nate. Take Harp and George along."

"It better look like an accident,"

muttered Earl, as he took off after Rocklin and Jardine.

Weems mopped his brow and, with Sturm and Gross following, led his horse out of the lamp-light. They stood close together on a dark patch of sidewalk, talking quietly.

"The Colorado job, three and a half years back," he muttered. "That Butterworth stage carrying the Symes and Cahill payroll."

"I ain't forgettin'," nodded Sturm. "The one time you got careless, Silky." He grinned scathingly. "Any man that can't tie a knot — so it won't slip . . . "

"All right," scowled Weems. "The damn kerchief came undone and one of the passengers saw my face."

"That same feller, huh?" prodded Grose. "The runt?"

"I remember I snapped a shot at him before we rode off," said Weems. "Later, when I read a newspaper story of the hold-up, I was sure I'd killed him. There was a passenger killed, but . . . "

"One of the others," frowned Sturm. "Not the galoot that saw you."

"He hasn't forgotten," said Weems, his voice shaking. "He recognized me — just as I recognized him. Of all the crazy luck . . . !"

"You can quit frettin'," opined Sturm. "With Nate at his heels, he's just never gonna talk to no tin star — nor anybody else."

"Silky, this could be a bad sign," mumbled Grose. "I ain't so sure we ought to go through with it. I mean — the town so crowded — and some galoot on the loose that could identify you. If one of us is caught — it won't be long before we all . . ."

"Listen, you gutless no-account!" snarled Weems, seizing him by his collar. "This had better be the last time you talk that way! I've had all I'll take of your whining!"

"Get a hold of yourself, Dace," advised Sturm. "Billy's worth a fortune to us, if Silky can figure how we're gonna steal him out of that jail. A fortune, Dace. We all worked for it, and you'll draw your share. But we gotta stick together, understand?"

"I ain't scared," protested Grose, pulling loose from the gambler. "And I ain't quittin' on you either. But, by Judas, things ain't goin' right. We gotta be careful — mighty careful."

Weems lit a cigar with trembling hands. They were staring along the street and the stogie was half-smoked when they sighted their three cohorts. At Weem's command, Sturm moved out to beckon them. The three paused to untie their horses and swing astride, then came on.

"Get mounted," ordered Weems. "I don't want to hear about it till we're well clear of town."

Some 10 minutes later, on the far fringe of the shanty town west of New Chance, they chose a campsite. While Jardine and Earl rigged a picket-line for the horses, Sturm gathered wood and got a fire going. Squatting on his blanket beside the fire, Weems listened eagerly to Rocklin's report.

"Soon as we caught up with him, I remembered," grinned the big man. "I was right beside you that day, Silky. That damn fancy scarf — you never tied it right . . ."

"I don't need to be reminded," muttered Weems. "Get to the point, Nate. Tell me what I need to hear."

"He didn't get time to turn you in," shrugged Rocklin. "I handled it fast and neat — and he made it easy for us. Tried to dodge us by sneakin into a side alley."

"You made sure nobody saw . . . ?" began Weems.

"Nobody saw," Rocklin assured him. "He never knew what hit him and, when he's found, nobody's gonna call it murder. I made damn sure of *that*."

"But how?" demanded Weems.

"It'll look like an accident," drawled Rocklin. "He was drunk, see? Fell and knocked himself out, flopped in a water trough and drowned."

"I don't like it," scowled Weems.

"Too elaborate. Too farfetched."

"You should worry," countered Rocklin. "Nobody saw us. There's just no way you could be tied into it." Grinning cheerfully, he suggested, "How about we break out the grub? I'm hungry."

"That's one problem done with," frowned Grose. "Now comes a bigger problem. Just how in blazes are we gonna take Billy out of that jail and right out of this pass — without gettin' our heads blowed off?"

"It'll take time and careful planning," said Weems, more at ease now. "We'll have to size up the situation, scout the jail and the area surrounding it, watch the routine of the guards . . ."

"And we'll have to get damn lucky," opined Rocklin.

"There'll be something," Weems promised. "A loophole. Some weakness in their routine — something we can use to our advantage."

"When do we start?" demanded Jardine, as he hunkered beside them.

"As soon as we've eaten, we'll stroll into the township," decided Weems. "Karl can stay with the horses while we take a look around."

"Just like all the other visitors, huh?" grinned Jardine.

"We'd better stay clear of that jailhouse," warned Grose. "For all we know, Billy could see us from his cell window. And — if he does . . . "

"That's the craziest thing you ever said, Dace," chided Jardine. "I swear you're so stiff-scared of Billy you ain't thinkin' straight. What have you got to fear from a hombre locked tight in a jail-cell?"

"Just knowin' he's that close," mumbled Grose, "makes my blood run cold."

In the crowded dining room at the New Chance Hotel, the Texans were finishing their supper, sharing a table with Hubert Quince. The fourth chair was reserved for Russ Newcombe, and now the gentle-voiced artist was offering a theory.

"He didn't show up for supper, and that puzzles you, Larry. Well, it shouldn't. He's a journalist after all, just as dedicated as his colleagues from the big cities. My guess is he talked his way into the jail again. Right now he's wheedling some answers from Marshal Hindmarsh."

"About that ruckus this mornin'?" challenged Stretch.

"Of course," nodded Quince.

"Seems to me Cyrus was mighty close-mouthed after the mayor untied him," said Larry.

"But Mister Newcombe — like reporters everywhere — can be very persuasive," opined Quince. "And what better time to interview the marshal?" He gestured to the other diners. "While the opposition has its nose in the feedbag."

"We'll likely catch up with him at the Eureka," shrugged Stretch.

As Molly Lamont arrived to collect their empty plates, Quince sat up straight and adjusted his necktie. He greeted her, as usual, with careful courtesy. And then, somewhat clumsily, he began his request.

"May I make so bold, Miss Molly — by your leave — and meaning no offense . . . "

"Land's sakes," she exclaimed, trading smiles with the Texans. "Have you ever heard a man so nervous?"

"Stay with it, Hubert boy," urged Stretch. "Take a couple deep breaths and try again."

"I was wondering — if it doesn't seem a liberty . . . " mumbled Quince.

"Wonderin' what?" asked Larry, his curiosity aroused.

"Stop wondering," Molly chided the artist. "Just ask."

"If you have some free time — say tomorrow," said Quince, "could we take a buggy-ride? I'm fascinated by the scenic grandeur of the Rockies and — perhaps you know of some — uh — peaceful spot . . . "

"Why, sure," she nodded. "I know the prettiest spring down along the western slopes, and it's not too far from town. I'll pack a basket. Must be a month of Sundays since you went on a picnic, Mister Quince, you being a city man."

"It seems ages," he confided wistfully. "Thank you, Miss Molly. I'll rent a vehicle and — shall we say eleven o'clock?"

"Eleven will be fine," said Molly. Having gathered the dishes, she took up her tray. "Enjoy your coffee, gentlemen." And then, on an afterthought, she flashed Quince an encouraging smile. "There now. That wasn't so difficult, was it?"

The Texans traded grins. Quince produced a handkerchief, dabbed at his moist brow and admitted to them,

"I have a lot to learn about women and how to court them. Never thought about it before. All these years, absorbed in my work, disinterested in the opposite sex. And now meeting this exceptional young lady — losing my head over her — I'm tongue-tied. To her I must seem twice as awkward as any westerner."

"Funny thing about our friend Hubert," Larry remarked.

"When that damn pencil's in his hand, he knows what he's about. Sketches up a dead ringer."

"Quicker'n you can wink," nodded Stretch.

"But, when it comes to somethin' easy — like sweet-talkin' a woman," said Larry, "he just don't know how to start."

"Thank you for putting it so bluntly," Quince said without rancor. "I needed that."

They were finishing coffee their coffee when Arnold Shell entered the dining room and made for their table. He was frowning uneasily and, even before he spoke, Larry's pulse was quickening.

"I thought you'd want to know, Valentine," muttered the hotelowner. "I'll have to tell all the others but, as you and Emerson seemed closely

159

acquainted, I'm telling you first. Your Texan friend — Russ Newcombe — is dead. They're taking the body to Oley Craydon's workshop behind the stage depot. An accident, they say. But a damn peculiar accident."

160

7

Post Mortem

THE reporters reached the clapboard building behind the stage depot hard on the heels of the Texans.

"Save your questions, gents," ordered Cyrus, as they crowded in. "Doc's checkin' the body now."

Larry stepped closer to the table where the body lay, but not close enough to impede the medico. The dead man's clothing was saturated. Their faces grim in the lamp-light, Jennings and company lined the walls and waited, some quietly trading comments.

"We scarce had time to get acquainted."

"Likeable little jasper. Didn't brag too much, though he had a right."

"Yeah. First man in. First out-of-towner to interview Reese."

Ten minutes passed before Doc retreated to the corner of the room to wash his hands. Nobody hustled him. For the first time since their arrival, the reporters showed restraint. Returning to the table, donning his coat, Doc tersely announced,

"Death by drowning."

"Drowned in a horse trough," frowned Cyrus. "First man I ever heard of to drown that way." To the reporters, he explained, "He was face-down in this trough in Kortner's Alley when a couple citizens found him. They hauled him out and sent for me, then we loaded him on a stretcher and brought him here."

"What two citizens?" demanded Jennings, opening his notebook.

"Me," offered Craydon. "And Dave Thorne. He's a drygoods drummer comes through every so often. We were takin' a short-cut through the alley. Mightn't have seen this feller if Dave hadn't stopped to light a cigar. It was real dark in there, and we were right beside the trough. Gave us one helluva shock, I'm tellin' you."

"Talk to Dave if you want," shrugged Cyrus. "I'll vouch for him. All the old hands know him."

"Accidental, huh Doc?" prodded Craydon. "He was drunk and . . . "

"That's a possibility," nodded Doc.

"Anybody know for sure?" Larry asked impatiently.

"Oley and Dave found an empty bottle by the trough," said Cyrus. "Of course — uh — that don't mean it had to be Mister Newcombe dropped it, but . . . "

"So it's only a conclusion," frowned Doc. "If you're interested, Larry, there's the bottle."

He gestured to the upturned box on which had been placed the contents of the dead man's pockets, his wallet, small change, handkerchief, notebook, pencil, cigars and matches and a few letters. Also a half-pint whiskey bottle.

"I already checked everything," offered Cyrus. "He wasn't robbed, if that's

163

what you're thinkin'. Hundred and eighty dollars in the wallet. Seventy-five cents in change."

"When the marshal said 'accident', you said 'possibility'," Freebold reminded the medico. "You got any doubts, Doc?"

"If Doc hasn't, *I* sure as hell have," growled Larry.

"Noticed it, did you?" challenged Doc. "You have a keen eye, my friend."

"What's Valentine talking about?" demanded Freebold.

"Did Newcombe fall into that trough and drown, or was he pushed?" asked Cleaver T. Harmon. Grimacing disdainfully, he added, "Either way it's a messy business."

"Cleave thinks even death ought to be neat and tidy," gibed Jennings.

"How about that mark on his jaw?" frowned Larry.

"Possibly Newcombe took a blow — possibly from a fist," Doc said guardedly. "On the other hand we can't rule out the possibility he suffered that

164

abrasion when he fell into the trough. The impact could have stunned him and . . . "

"And then he fell into cold water and didn't come to his senses," muttered Larry. "Just flopped and drowned."

"You're sceptical," observed Doc.

"So are you," countered Larry.

"Well, Doc?" challenged McWhirter.

"Larry has made a point," said Doc. "If Mister Newcombe's death wasn't accidental . . . "

"Only one other way it could happen," Larry said grimly. "He was clobbered, shoved into the trough and held down. He drowned, sure, but it wasn't his idea."

"Speculation," Harmon said loftily.

Stretch glanced sidelong at the New Yorker the while he finished rolling a cigarette.

"Mister, I've been knocked off of my horse by a bullet and fell in a river," he drawled. "Hurt and weak from bleedin', you know? But I stayed wide awake."

"Shock of cold water," said Jennings, nodding knowingly.

"But we *are* speculating, Larry," said Doc. "So, as unofficial coroner of New Chance, my verdict will have to be death by misadventure."

"He was one of us — a newspaperman — and maybe it was murder," said Jennings. "I'm speaking for all my colleagues here . . . "

"And demanding a full investigation," guessed Doc.

"That's the least Newcombe's entitled to," opined Freebold.

"I got two good men guardin' Reese," announced Cyrus, "so I'm free to check into this thing. Can't make no promises, but I'll sure do my best."

"How will you start?" wondered Quince.

"A lot of walkin' and a lot of talkin'," shrugged Cyrus. "I move around and ask question, and maybe some citizen saw Newcombe — and maybe he wasn't alone. That's the first thing I'll try to

166

find out." On his way from the room, he added, "Best get started."

Stretch lit his cigarette and ambled across to study the items on the upturned box. Larry, after a last long glance at the dead man's face, asked the medico,

"Will he be shipped back to Denver?"

"He'll have to be buried here — and no later than tomorrow afternoon," said Doc. "More than enough in his wallet to pay for a decent funeral. I'll have Jerry wire the news to the Clarion editor, but, if Newcombe had any family, there's no way they could travel from Denver to New Chance in time for the funeral."

"We're better than two hundred and fifty miles from Denver as the crow flies," Craydon pointed out. "And no direct route."

"Of course the balance of the cash will be mailed to his editor," said Doc, donning his hat. "You'll take over now, Oley?"

The reporters made their exit slowly,

the Texans following. Outside, Jennings lit a cigar, sighed heavily and remarked to his colleagues,

"Journalists are callous sons-of-bitches — present company included."

"Now see here, Jennings . . ." began Harmon.

"Get off your high horse, Cleave," chided Jennings. "You were just another blood-sniffing, low-paid scribbler before they gave you a by-line and made you a feature-writer. So you know damn well what I mean. If a Chicago cop is murdered, the whole damn police department works night and day to find the killer. It's the same in New York."

"And 'Frisco," nodded Freebold.

"But a reporter doesn't rate so high," Jennings said bitterly. "We'll wire our editors the news of Newcombe's death and do a two-paragraph follow-up — and that's all."

"Take it easy, Sam," muttered Freebold. "A bunch of newspapermen can't transform themselves into a force of trained investigators. Nosing out the story is our game. Apprehending killers is a lawman's responsibility."

"Every man to his trade, Jennings," frowned Bennett. "How'd you feel if some desk-sergeant in some Chigago precinct wrote a news story? How'd you feel if your editor bought it — and printed it?"

"Well," shrugged Jennings, "when you put it that way . . . "

"Maybe I should've fetched my camera," suggested Kress.

About to move away, the Texans jerked to a halt, glowering at him.

"What was that you said?" challenged Larry.

"I'm talking about a picture of the corpus delecti," the photographer explained. "It's routine nowadays. Well, certainly in the big cities, cowboy. Readers expect it."

"Feller comes up dead — and you take his pictures?" prodded Stretch.

"Why not?" demanded Kress.

Larry jerked a thumb toward

Craydon's workshop and said bluntly,

"If I learn you've photographed Newcombe, I'll break your damn-blasted camera — and your head along with it."

"And, if Larry don't, *I* will," warned Stretch.

"Well, damnitall . . . !" began McWhirter.

"I didn't make a sketch of the body," Quince pointed out. "I suppose I share their attitude. I just felt . . . " He shrugged uncomfortably, "Newcombe's entitled to privacy — and respect."

"You guys hardly knew Newcombe," argued Jennings.

"He was a Texan," said Larry.

"Which means he was a friend of ours," said Stretch.

The drifters strode away and, staring after them, Jennings confided to the other reporters,

"When they said 'Texan', it was as if we should genuflect."

On their way to the Eureka, the Texans stopped by the dark alley where the Denver reporter had died. They checked the area by match-light, Larry moodily studying the trough and the disturbed ground.

"About that bottle," he muttered.

"Colonel's Favorite," offered Stretch. "We've killed many a bottle runt but I don't recollect that brand."

"We'll ask Jake," Larry decided, as they quit the alley. "And, if he can't help us, we'll check every bar in town."

"We won't be leavin' New Chance, huh?" prodded Stretch.

"We got unfinished business," growled Larry.

"Little Russ," nodded Stretch.

"If he died accidental," said Larry, "I'll quit driftin' and start raisin' hogs."

"We're strangers in this territory and so was Russ," Stretch pointed out. "He didn't have time to make no enemies, and he wasn't robbed. So the whole lousy deal is plumb mysterious — and you ain't gonna let up."

"Not so you'd notice," said Larry. "I want the polecat that drowned him."

"If he's still here."

"I can't swear he's still here. But I got a hunch."

"So here we go again — huntin' a killer. And you don't even know where to start."

"Only one way to start," declared Larry. "Find out *why* he was killed. When I learn the reason, I'll know what kind of polecat to look for."

Reaching the saloon, they shouldered their way through the night-crowd to find elbow-propping space at the bar and catch Jake Sharney's eye. He limped along to them and, without asking their order, poured two stiff shots of rye.

"I heard about Newcombe," he said sadly. "The news is all over town. Helluva way for a man to go." They worked on their whiskey a few moments before Larry put his question. Jake sniffed in disapproval. "Colonel's Favorite? Sure, I've heard of it. But I'd never serve it, and Roscoe would never have it in the place. Cheap rot-gut.

172

No better than snakehead moonshine. I don't recall I've ever seen a bottle in New Chance, even when the old town was boomin'."

"We'll have to make sure," frowned Larry.

"Meanin' we check every bar in town," guessed Stretch.

"You gonna tell me why?" asked Jake.

"Empty bottle by the trough where they found Russ," Larry said tersely. "Colonel's Favorite."

"Started diggin' already, have you?" challenged Jake.

"If no local saloon is sellin' that stuff . . . " began Larry.

"Yeah, I know," nodded Jake. "It'll mean the bottle was brought in by a visitor — and New Chance is crawlin' with visitors right now. And where will that leave you? How can you be sure the bottle was dropped by Newcombe's killer?"

"He said 'killer'," remarked Stretch.

"I was a lawman a long time,"

shrugged Jake. "Men like Newcombe don't flop and drown in horse-troughs. That kind of accident I don't buy. So — anything I can do to help — anything at all . . ."

"Much obliged," said Larry.

The Texans downed their drinks and were about to say good-night, when the ex-lawman muttered another comment.

"Helluva way to do a man. If I didn't know he was jail-bound, *he'd* be my first suspect."

"Reese?" prodded Larry.

"Sometimes he didn't kill fast," growled Jake. "Sometimes he'd figure some crazy way. Like, for instance, the homesteader in Corbett, Utah. He smothered that poor galoot. They found him in a near-dry creekbed — his face pressed tight into the mud."

The drifters gave no further thought to Jake Sharney's words until they had canvassed every saloon and drawn a blank.

"That's plain loco," Stretch protested,

when Larry decided their next move. "If Reese got out, the whole town'd be jumpin'. And, if he got out and killed Russ, would he sneak back to his cell? And how could he get past them guards?"

"Let's just say I'm curious," drawled Larry. "Curious enough to take a close look at a skunk who kills for pleasure."

Cyrus Hindmarsh, footsore and disgruntled, was returning to his office when they hailed him. As they drew closer, the guards on the porch rose from their chairs and cocked their shotguns.

"It's okay," grunted the lawman. "I know these two. Valentine — Emerson — somethin' I can do for you?"

"You had any luck?" asked Larry, as they followed him into the office.

"Plenty," scowled Cyrus. "All bad. Nobody saw nothin'. Well, what can you expect? The town's damn near as busy as when the mines were open and the stamp mill goin' full blast. Main Street's so crowded a man could be knifed, flop and get walked over — and nobody the wiser."

"This place got a back door?" demanded Larry.

"Uh huh." Cyrus nodded warily. "Locked and barred. Why?"

"How about those cell-locks upstairs?" prodded Stretch. "You check 'em regular?"

"Listen now," frowned Cyrus. "Them locks . . ."

"I got a sudden urge to take another look at Billy Reese," said Larry. "And I don't reckon you'll object."

"Seein' as how . . ." Stretch grinned and winked, "Ol, Larry kinda helped you arrest him — in a manner of speakin'."

"You could check the locks while we're lookin' him over," suggested Larry.

"I guess I owe you that much," conceded Cyrus, unhitching his key-ring.

He led them upstairs and along to the occupied cell. At their arrival, the prisoner swung his feet to the floor and rose to a sitting position to eye them cautiously. Cyrus checked the lock of that cell and all the others, while Appleyard and the Texans matched stares.

"More snoopers," jeered Appleyard. "Here for a close look at Bloody Billy, huh?"

"Remember me?" challenged Larry.

"Yeah." Appleyard averted his gaze. "I remember you."

"I'd never have guessed it," drawled Larry. "Reese the badman, the trigger-happy killer, wantin' to blow his brains out — because of a woman."

"You couldn't understand," declared Appleyard, and now his voice had a whinning quality. "She was the one girl I . . . " He checked himself abruptly. Cyrus was joining the Texans, eyeing him warningly. "Aw, forget it. I ain't supposed to talk about her."

"Howzat again?" frowned Stretch.

"I mean — I don't *wanta* talk about her," muttered Appleyard. He worked up a defiant grin and asserted, "It'll be more fun talkin' about all the fools I've killed, all the dumb deputies and stagecoach guards and . . ."

"Whistlin' in the dark, Billy?" gibed Larry. "You'd as soon brag than admit you're scared?"

"Don't provoke him, Valentine," chided Cyrus.

"I don't scare that easy," growled Appleyard. "That's why I'm the meanest, the toughest . . ."

"Let's get out of here," said Larry.

Cyrus followed the Texans downstairs, a mite unsettled, but choosing his words with care.

"No way he could get out of his cell — let alone sneak back again. I've checked every lock, and it just ain't possible."

"Yeah, sure," grunted Larry, nodding absently.

"I don't savvy you, Valentine," said the lawman. "Them big city reporters got good reason for talkin' to my prisoner, writin' about him. That's

178

their trade. But why *you* wanted to see him — and talk to him that way — I just don't savvy."

"Just curiosity," shrugged Larry.

"He's always curious," offered Stretch, "about hombres that want to be dead."

From the jailhouse, the tall men dawdled to the hotel. They paused while crossing Main to avoid a passing rider, an unkempt jasper with long black hair and beard, rigged in the rough garb of a trapper and leading a laden pack-horse. Absorbed in their conversation, they spared the newcomer no more than a brief glance.

"You got somethin' else on your mind now. I mean, as well as Russ Newcombe," muttered Stretch, when they reached the opposite sidewalk. "I could tell. Up in the jailhouse, while you were swappin' gab with Billy."

"Somethin's wrong," Larry said pensively. "Somethin' don't add up right. But, if I talked it around, every galoot'd claim I'm out of my mind."

"So try it on me," urged Stretch. "If I think you're out of your mind, I'll sure tell you."

"Thanks a heap," grunted Larry.

"What's a friend for?" shrugged Stretch. "C'mon now. What don't add up right?"

"I guess I was leery at the start," confided Larry. "Right after they'd locked that jasper up and spread the word they'd captured a dangerous bandido. To me it sounded kind of far-fetched, but I wasn't about to argue. If an outlaw gets to pinin' for some female and tries to shoot himself, no skin off my nose."

"But . . . ?" prodded Stretch.

"We've heard a lot of talk about Reese since they turned the key on him," Larry pointed out. "Worst badman of all, they say. Kills for the pleasure of it."

"That's what they say," agreed Stretch. "But you ain't satisfied?"

"That's it," nodded Larry. "I ain't satisfied. And I'm startin' to

180

wonder — have they got the right man, the real Billy Reese?"

"He's *gotta* be the real Billy!" frowned Stretch. "Hell, runt, he's braggin' of all the folks he butchered. He knows he's gallows-bait. So, if he ain't Billy, why would he claim he *is* Billy?"

"That's what I don't understand," said Larry. "But I'm still leery. You recall how he said he wasn't supposed to talk of his girl? And then, sudden-like, he put it another way, said he didn't *want* to talk of her."

"That's important?" challenged Stretch.

"When a man says he ain't supposed to do somethin', it could mean he's under orders," suggested Larry.

"Well, maybe so," shrugged Stretch. "But, doggone it, no man could order him to say he's Billy Reese — if he ain't."

"I guess not," sighed Larry, as they moved into the hotel.

"So now what?" demanded Stretch.

"So I'll keep on frettin' about it,"

181

Larry said irritably.

Milo Tweedy was thinking of closing up when the stranger appeared in his doorway, hefting a bundle of pelts. After supper trade had been brisk — and profitable — but the last customer had come and gone 20 minutes before.

"Make me a good price and they're yours," offered Reese, dumping his bundle on the counter.

"Well . . . " began Tweedy.

"Take your time. Look 'em over," urged Reese. "I'll settle for what's fair."

"I don't know," frowned Tweedy. "Not much demand for . . . "

"Hogwash," jeered Reese, helping himself to an apple from the barrel by the pot-bellied stove. "On my way in, I saw a whole crowd of easterners, greenhorns in city clothes. You know they'll buy damn near anything — in the town where Billy Reese is gonna hang."

"Before he hangs he'll have a fair

trial," Tweedy hastened to point out. "I'm not just the owner of this store, Mister . . . ?"

"Billings. Jim Billings."

"Well now, Mister Billings, I happen to be mayor of New Chance, and you can take it from me. The law will be upheld. Bloody Billy will have his day in court."

"Bad medicine, the way I hear it." Reese propped an elbow on the counter, bit into his apple and watched Tweedy examine the skins. "Must've put up one helluva fight, huh?"

"There was no fight, I'm proud to say," drawled the mayor. "Our gallant Marshal Hindmarsh recognized Reese in a saloon, challenged him and got the drop."

"Got the drop on Billy Reese?" The stranger shook his head in wonderment. "Beat Billy's fast draw?"

"I wish I'd seen it," said Tweedy, grinning blandly. "Witnesses claim the marshal's gun was out and cocked before Reese's hand reached his holster."

"I wish *I'd* seen it," Reese said fervently.

"About these skins," said Tweedy. "I've seen better."

"You've seen worse," countered Reese. "Make me an offer — but don't get greedy, Mister Mayor. We wouldn't want to wrangle, would we?" Tweedy named a price. Reese leered at him. "I calculate that's thirty dollars less'n what they're worth. Now you think about it, huh? Think of how you'll up your price on every skin and make yourself a fat profit."

"You strike a hard bargain, Billings," complained Tweedy, reaching into his till. "Very well." He counted out the money. "There it is — plus the extra thirty." His avaricious nerves tingled as Reese snatched the wad and stowed it in a pocket. "And now — I'm sure you'll be needin' supplies. Anything you want, you'll find it right here . . . "

"At your price," gibed Reese, turning toward the door. "No thanks. I'm here to rest my animals a while. Not to make you rich."

Moving along Main, leading the saddler and the pack-horse, he chuckled inwardly, childishly pleased at having outsmarted the storekeeper. Before seeking a campsite, he traveled past the town jail and stared up to a yellow square in its grim facade, the window of the occupied cell.

"That'll be where he's stashed," he reflected. "The fool they claim is me. Yeah, he'd have to be a fool."

His sardonic humor gave way to cold fury when he glimpsed the half-completed gallows in Bonanza Road. En route to New Chance he had been grimly amused at the prospect of attending the trial, execution and burial of Billy Reese as an onlooker. Now, studying that ugly framework of beams and planks silhouetted in the moonlight, he mumbled curses on the town's civic leaders and all the riff-raff gathering to witness the inglorious end of a notorious boss-outlaw.

This was to be one of those times feared by his cohorts of the past, a time when his behaviour was downright irrational. But, though in the grip of his emotions, he maintained his animal cunning.

Patiently, he scouted the area between New Chance's south side and the towering rock-wall of the pass. The campsite he chose was well-removed from his nearest neighbors, a party of drifting cowpokes who had rigged lean-to's some 45 yards away. Until 3 a.m. he rested. And then, with the town wrapped in its pre-dawn silence, he rose and made his way back to the Tweedy Emporium.

Picking the padlock of Tweedy's storehouse was an easy chore. From that building, located across the alley from the emporium, he crept to Bonanza Road, toting a can of coal-oil.

8

Stalk, Kill and Stalk Again

AT 3.20 a.m., the clamor began along Main Street.

The clanging of a bell and a confusion of wild yells and shouted commands roused the occupants of buildings lining the main stem and, in particular, the guests of the New Chance Hotel. Larry and Stretch, yawning and grouching, quit their beds, dashed cold water into their eyes and began dressing; the disturbance was probably none of their business, but old habits die hard.

When they emerged from their room, they were caught up and carried along by a dozen or more reporters in varying stages of undress. If trouble-shooters reacted instinctively, so did gentlemen of the press.

"Well, who cares if there *is* a fire?" grumbled McWhirter. "How do we know it's worth covering? Some damn rube could've set fire to his own lavatory!"

"You're in the West now, partner," quipped Freebold. "Out here, they call it a privy."

"Leo, gimme a hand with this camera for pity's sakes!" gasped Kress. "Any fire in this town is news. Harrigan's bound to want a picture."

"Got a pencil, Quince?" demanded Jennings.

"Always," yawned Quince.

Along Main to the corner of Bonanza dashed the crowd of locals and visitors, there to gape at the fiery spectacle. As bright as day, the glow of it illuminated that end of Bonanza and a half-block of Main. The onlookers enjoyed a clear view of the blazing framework of the gallows, the scurrying bucket brigade hurling water in a vain bid to save the structure, the mayor and his fellow councilmen grouped on the sidewalk, angrily denouncing this act of arson.

"Wanton vandalism!" raged Tweedy. "Wilful destruction of what was to become a historic edifice! This was no accident, damnitall! Some rogue started this fire deliberate!"

"A symbolic gesture of protest," Jennings wrote into his notebook. "New Chance, scene of the Reese trial, has its own anti-hanging faction, an organization whose members are as yet unknown to the local authorities . . . "

Nearby, Barney Freebold of the San Francisco Dispatch was scribbling,

"Time and time again, New Chance's gallant fire-fighters charged the conflagration. Fire-Chief Winthrop J. Hickok, a distant relative of the legendary Wild Bill, persisted valiantly until his men carried him free with his clothes afire. Their prompt action saved his life. They immersed him in a water trough . . . "

He flinched in exasperation as Bennett, the Ohio man, muttered a challenge.

"Who the hell is Fire-Chief Hickok?

There's no regular fire brigade here, and no galoot's been dunked in a trough with his pants a'blaze."

"You ought to know better than to read over a man's shoulder," chided Freebold. "I invented the Chief, of course. Literary licence, Bennett."

"You're some helluva fiction writer — I'll say that for you," grinned Bennett.

"In 'Frisco, who'd know anyway?" countered Freebold.

Wrote Leo McWhirter, bleary-eyed, only half-awake, but a sensationalist to the core,

"Civil authorities, led by Mayor Milo Tweedy and the intrepid Marshal Hindmush, began their investigation while the fire still raged along Banana Road. Menanced by the spreading inferno, men, women, children and others fled their homes in their night attire. A half-breed Indian woman was shocked into early labor and gave birth to a nine-pound baby boy. It is suspected the father is none other than Billy Reese himself. In an exclusive statement to this reporter, the notorious gunman admitted his reason for risking capture here in New Chance was strictly personal . . . "

"They'll never save it!" groaned Tweedy, as blazing beams began sagging.

"Keep your shirt on," growled Lippert. "We aren't short of lumber. They can start building a new gallows first thing tomorrow. And, meanwhile, the reporters are happy. No danger they'll lose interest."

Watching from his vantagepoint, the top step of a nearby building, Reese scanned the excited crowd. His low-hanging hair and thick beard concealed his complacent grin. More than satisfied with his handiwork and its aftermath, he was about to change position when, clearly illuminated on the edge of the throng, he sighted and recognized two familiar faces.

"The hell with 'em! Jardine and Grose! And, if they're here, the rest can't be far away!"

More elated than alarmed, he concentrated on the two, following their movements. Grose, after a few moments, seemed to lose interest in the fire. He nudged Jardine, who shook his head. Shrugging, Grose turned and moved away. And then Reese moved, descending from the steps and maneuvering to get closer to the burly hard case.

When, at last, Jardine moved away from the scene, Reese was almost close enough to touch him. Unsuspecting, Jardine turned into an alley angling off Bonanza Road and signed his own death warrant; he was always wary of crowds, and the main stem was jam-packed now.

Half-way along the alley, he sensed he was being followed. His hand dropped to his holster, but too late. Reese's left arm locked about his neck from behind, jerking his head back. The Colt came free of leather, but with Reese's right hand gripping Jardine's wrist like a vice.

"Yeah, Harp, it's me!" Reese whispered into his ear. "Takes more'n fire and dynamite to kill Billy. Oh, sure. But you now, Harp. You're good as dead!"

In his last moments, Jardine suffered the horror of feeling his own pistol turned toward him. He was strong, but Reese was stronger. Struggle as he might, he couldn't free himself.

Blazing planks and beams collapsed while Tweedy, the reporters and the Texans watched helplessly. It was Oley Craydon who whirled and pointed and announced,

"Hey! I just heard a shot — over there somewhere!"

"I didn't hear anything," scowled Tweedy.

"Who could hear a shot over all that din?" challenged Cyrus.

"If somebody got shot, I don't want to know about it," Doc Bayes said impatiently. "No fool suffered burns, so there's nothing to keep me from my bed."

"I *did* hear a shot!" insisted Craydon.

"Listen, I couldn't swear to it, but I heard something too," offered Jerry Webb. "And — uh — it might have been a gun."

"A fire makes good copy," remarked Jennings. "But a shooting is even better. You gonna investigate, Marshal?"

"We'll all come along," announced Freebold.

"You hear anything, runt?" asked Stretch, as the civic leaders moved past the ruin of the gallows with the reporters in tow.

"I'm not sure," shrugged Larry. "So we might's well tag along."

"Oh, well," sighed Doc. "Just in case . . ."

"In here, it sounded like," muttered Craydon, leading them into the alley.

Moments later, Cyrus and Craydon stumbled over the huddled body. Lippert bellowed for somebody to fetch a lamp and Webb dashed into a nearby building.

"Stand back, everybody!" ordered

Tweedy. "Get a move on, Jerry!"

"Anybody got a match?" asked the telegrapher.

"Thunderation! What is this — a stampede?" gasped Doc, as a half-dozen inquisitive locals barged past him. "Let me through, confound you!"

Somebody got the lamp working and, in its glow, the dead outlaw was clearly revealed — a sight to shock the locals, arouse the Texans' interest and start the visiting journalists scribbling again. The body was in a squatting position. Jardine had died with his face upturned, eyes and mouth open, an expression of abject terror stamped on his face. His clothing smoldered around his mortal wound, the ugly hole in his chest. The discharged Colt was still gripped in his right hand.

Tweedy voiced the obvious conclusion. "Suicide! Shot himself with his own gun!" To that he added a bitter complaint. "Why'd he have to do it in *my* town?"

"The Reese hanging was all you

195

counted on, huh Mayor?" grinned Jennings.

"You sore at this galoot for stealing Reese's thunder?" challenged Freebold.

"I'll have to identify him somehow." As Cyrus said that, he glanced at the onlookers, one of whom was beginning a hasty retreat. "Hey! Stop that jasper! Bring him back here!"

"Gettin' jumpy, ain't you, Cyrus?" frowned Craydon. "Plain enough this feller killed himself, so you don't have to look for no killer."

"Sure it's suicide." The marshal nodded impatiently. "But it's my job to identify him — and I've seen him with that skinny hombre." He stared hard at Dacey Grose, reluctantly coming to the fore with two hefty locals prodding him. "Yeah, you're the one. I spotted you runnin' along Main with him when I come out of my office."

"No law against that, is there?" mumbled Grose. "Everybody was runnin'. We got curious and tagged along."

196

"But you knew him," Larry interjected.

"Hold on now, Valentine, I'll handle this," chided Cyrus.

"I've just remembered I saw you with him," said Larry, nodding to the body. "You were watchin' the fire, talkin' together like old buddies."

"Well, that's all true enough," said Grose. In this time of shock and fear, he was clinging to his nerve, forcing himself to devise answers to satisfy the lawman and preserve his anonymity. "Part true anyway. I came along the street with him, sure, and I was with him, lookin' at the fire. But there ain't much I can tell you about him. We met along the trail, ridin' into New Chance."

"You must've known his name," insisted Cyrus.

"Jar — I mean Jay . . ." faltered Grose. "His name was Jay Dean."

"And you?" demanded Cyrus.

"Dacey. Sid Dacey." Grose shrugged uneasily. "I scarce knew him at all, Marshal. He was practically a stranger to me. All I learned was his name. Just wasn't enough time for us to get close acquainted."

"Must've pressed the muzzle against his chest before he pulled the trigger," observed McWhirter. "The gunflash started his shirt and jacket burning."

"Thank you, Detective McWhirter," grinned Freebold. "No need for a post mortem this time, huh Doc? Clear case of suicide?"

"I'll make a closer examination in Oley's workshop," decided Doc, rising from beside the body.

"You couldn't have any doubts," protested Lippert.

"My responsibility, Roscoe," said Doc. "I'm supposed to make absolutely sure."

"Sure of what?" challenged Tweedy. "He's dead and we know how he died — by his own hand — so what else d'you want?"

"Call it idle curiosity if you like," muttered Doc.

"And just what are you curious

about, Doc?" prodded Jennings.

"The expression on his face," said Doc.

The reporters leaned forward for a closer look.

"Poor guy was terrified — not much doubt about that," observed Bennett. "Well, who *wouldn't* be?"

"How else could a man feel — while killing himself?" shrugged McWhirter.

"I've always had the idea a suicide is uncommonly brave," Doc said thoughtfully, "or out of his mind."

"You through with me?" Grose asked Cyrus. "Nothin' more I can tell you."

"All right, you can go," nodded Cyrus. "C'mon, Oley, I'll help you tote him to your workshop."

"This is more than I counted on," muttered Craydon, as he bent to grasp the dead man's legs. "I was all ready to take care of Reese, but that's all. This is the second in a few hours. Two funerals this afternoon . . . "

Doc Bayes worked with his customary thoroughness, managing to suppress his resentment; he felt like a performer surrounded by an audience. Craydon's makeshift funeral parlor was crowded. Larry and Stretch had followed the civic leaders in, and the reporters were close behind. But strict silence was observed, the onlookers lining the walls to give the medico elbow room. The Texans found themselves pressed against the closed casket containing the mortal remains of Russell Newcombe. And Larry, always a hunch-player, saw this as an omen. It was as though the hapless, sawn-off Texan were jogging his memory. His murder had been disguised as an accident, and now another had died, this time a supposed suicide.

Doc began by removing the upper garments, revealing the dead man's torso, the ugly wound in the hairy chest, the limp bare arms. Cyrus moved forward to check the pockets of shirt and jacket, while Doc covered the face; the expression stamped thereon was plaguing his nerves. The right hand was raised to rest on the belt-buckle, and it was then that Doc bluntly announced,

"I'm calling it murder."

Some of the reporters loosed startled oaths. The mayor, waving his arms in exasperation, hurled a challenge.

"Now how in blazes are you gonna make murder out of suicide — when we found this man the way we did — his gun still in hs hand . . . "

"You can all move closer, see for yourself," offered Doc. As they obeyed, he lifted the right forearm. "Observe the wrist, gentlemen. Extensive bruising. The clear impression of a thumb and fingers — indicating what should be obvious."

"You mean . . . ?" began Lippert.

"I'd say he was seized from behind," said Doc. "His assailant may have pinned his other arm, or he could have hooked his left arm about Dean's neck. If he were powerful enough — and we can assume he was — Dean's head would be forced back. The killer captured Dean's right wrist, maybe before, maybe after the pistol was drawn."

"Well, by golly, if his hand was bigger'n Dean's . . . !" frowned Cyrus.

"More likely it was Dean cocked the gun," muttered Larry.

"You sound mighty sure about that," said McWhirter.

"His holster was tied down — like mine," Larry pointed out.

"For a fast draw," nodded Freebold. Grinning smugly at Kress, he remarked, "I'm learning."

"Any man pulls a gun in a hurry," explained Larry, "he thumbs the hammer back while he's clearin' leather."

"But, with his own gun prodding his chest, Dean wouldn't be fool enough to jerk the trigger," frowned Lippert.

"If it was me, I'd have dropped the damn thing," muttered Cyrus.

"You're thinking clearly," countered Doc. "Dean was in shock. Anyway, with the muzzle pressed against his victim, the killer only needed to shift his grip. By wrapping his hand around Dean's, he caused the weapon to discharge. And, any way you look at it, that's murder."

"Well — Lawd almighty!" gasped Craydon. "What a way to kill a man!"

"Some kind of maniac's on the loose!" announced Freebold, shuddering.

"We don't know what trade this guy worked at, but we sure know about Newcombe," said McWhirter. "Hell! He was one of us!"

"You saying this maniac's got a special grudge against newspapermen?" challenged Bennett.

"It's possible," asserted McWhirter. "And I'm no hero. I'm an individualist dedicated to my own welfare and the San Francisco Herald — in that order. Mayor Tweedy, what's your price for a pistol — loaded?"

"You got a Smith and Wesson in stock?" Jennings asked urgently. "Short-barreled — about the size of a hip pocket?"

"I want to buy a derringer," announced Freebold.

"Not powerful enough," said Kress.

"Baloney!" retorted Freebold. "How do you think Booth killed Lincoln — with a shotgun?"

"I'll settle for *any* kind of gun!" wailed McWhirter. "As long as it can blow a hole through the lunatic who killed Newcombe and Dean!"

The sudden exodus began in disorderly fashion. Milo Tweedy was more than willing to open his store and sell a dozen or more handguns at an exorbitant price, but wasn't given time to say so; he was seized by Jennings, McWhirter and Freebold and almost carried out with the other newsmen following. Only Quince remained with Doc and the Texans. The other councilmen had left — Cyrus to begin an abortive search for clues to the identity of the assassin.

"We welcomed those big-shot journalists," Doc said sadly, as he covered the body. "We were so damn grateful to see them, because New Chance was dying on its feet for want of publicity — fame — notoriety."

"And Billy Reese came along, right when you needed him," drawled Larry.

"But this is more than we counted on," sighed Doc. "TWO UNSOLVED MURDERS. Damn it, if there's a third, we'll *lose* those reporters. They came here for a big story — not to get shot at by some homicidal idiot, or drowned in a horse trough."

"Taking a great deal for granted, aren't you?" Quince gently suggested, as they moved out. "Why assume both murders were committed by the same man? I see no connection, nothing to indicate . . ."

"Great Caesar's ghost!" gasped Doc. "*Two* killers at large?"

"Who can say?" shrugged Quince.

"I guess Hubert's got a point," mused Stretch.

"If there are two of 'em, I only want the one that butchered little Russ," growled Larry.

The gallows was nought but a tangle of smoldering rubble now and Main Street almost deserted again, most of the population having returned to their beds.

In his camp west of the township, Billy Reese wrapped himself in his blankets and, before lapsing into slumber, did some deep thinking. Following Grose had proved an easy chore; a score or more transients were retreating to the west end of the pass when the nervous outlaw quit the murder scene. Grose had joined the moving throng and Reese had kept him in sight, tagging him to where his cohorts were camped.

"All of 'em," he reflected, yawning contentedly. "All squattin' around a fire and lookin' plenty fazed. Silky and Nate, Karl and George and that yellow-bellied Dacey Grose. But not Harp. Hell, no. One down — five to go. Plain enough why they're here. Hopin' to find me and make me talk. Hungerin' for the loot. And that's funny. There ain't no loot, and maybe I'll tell 'em — before I pick 'em off — one by one . . . "

206

At this moment, Silky Weems was drawing a flaming stick from the fire to light a cigar. Hunkered either side of him, Rocklin and Earl scowled impatiently at the haggard Dacey Grose. Sturm, bored but not dismayed, filled the coffeepot and set it on the fire.

"So Harp got it," he grunted. "That's rough, but there ain't nothin' we can do about it."

"And Billy's in jail and under tight guard," muttered Rocklin.

"Yeah, I know that," nodded Grose. "But, hell, Silky . . . " In his eagerness to convince the gambler he became incoherent. "How do we know — I mean — Billy might've found somebody else. It's been three years, so he's had time . . . "

"Exactly what the hell *are* you talking about?" challenged Weems.

"Billy scarce ever worked alone." Grose disciplined himself to speak slowly. "Maybe he's got new friends. He's in jail, but they're free. And they're right here. If he saw us from that cell-window — and passed the word to 'em . . ."

"I don't believe that's possible," Weems said curtly.

"We'll never know who killed Harp — or why," shrugged Rocklin. "Only thing we can be sure of is Harp would never kill himself."

"Some hard case jumped Harp in the alley," opined Earl. "Harp put up a fight, started pullin' his gun and the feller panicked and made a grab for it. Damn gun was cocked and Harp's luck ran out, that's all. As for the galoot that jumped him — he's still runnin'."

"We've lost a man, but nothing's changed," said Weems. "We're here for a showdown with that crazy double-crosser and, one way or nother, we have to get him away from that jail."

When Milo Tweedy closed up again, the reporters hustled along to the Western Union office where Jerry Webb, anticipating their wishes, had donned his clothes, stoked up his stove and opened his transmitter. Jennings and his colleagues, their pockets sagging from the weight of their newly-purchased pistols, crowded the counter and clamored for message forms. Within the hour, New York, Chicago, San Francisco and Dayton, Ohio editors were advised of the second violent death and the destruction of the gallows.

At breakfast in the dining room of the hotel, the guests were red-eyed from lack of sleep, and the Lone Star Hellions were no exception. But their appetite was unaffected. Sharing a table by a front window, they worked steadily on the ham, eggs and hot biscuits served them by Molly Lamont.

Sam Jennings, last to arrive, made his way to their table and was invited to join them.

"Just coffee — black," he told Molly as he seated himself.

"Where's your picture-drawin' side-kick?" enquired Stretch.

"Sleeping like a babe — lucky

209

Hubert," sighed Jennings. "I swear nothing worries that boy. The artistic instinct, I guess. Only time I've seen him sweat was when he got his first eyeful of the little lady." He glanced after Molly. "Well, that proves he's got good taste."

"No argument," shrugged Larry.

"You're getting around a handsome breakfast," Jennings wistfully observed. "And all I can eat is humble pie. Boy! Is my face red!"

"Somethin' wrong?" asked Stretch.

"My memory's failing, and that's a failure no journalist can afford," declared Jennings. "All this time I've been rubbing shoulders with a couple of living legends and didn't realize it, didn't remember where or how I'd heard the names before — until I woke up this morning." He stared hard at Larry. "Valentine and Emerson, the famous Texas Hell-Raisers. You look exactly like your photographs — and *still* I didn't recognize you."

"Do yourself a favor," advised Larry.

"Forget you know who we are."

"Take it easy," soothed Jennings. "What could be written about you that *hasn't* been written? And, besides, I'm here for the Billy Reese story." He muttered his thanks as Molly delivered his coffee. "You're looking pretty as ever this morning, Miss Molly. And, in answer to your unspoken question, Quince is fast asleep."

"How did you know I was about to ask . . . ?" she began.

"I'm an expert mind-reader," he quipped.

"'Cept when you're in a poker game," taunted Stretch.

Molly moved away smiling, while Jennings grimaced ruefully and declared, "That hurt. I felt it — right here." He patted the pocket containing his wallet. "Well, like I said, I'm eating humble pie."

"He's just another scribbler," Stretch remarked to Larry. "But one thing you can say for him. He's no sore loser."

"We'll all turn out for Russ

Newcombe's funeral this afternoon," said Jennings, after his first mouthful of coffee. "You know, I keep thinking about the little guy. Texas-born — that right?" Larry nodded slowly. "Sure. But just as much a regular newspaperman as any I know in Chicago." He winced and confided, "I'm sorry now. Sorry I didn't get to know him better. And sorry I doubted his word. He bragged a little, sure, but who am I to say he was kidding us? It could've been the gospel truth. I mean, Colorado was his beat, so it could've happened just the way he told us."

"Little Russ — braggin'?" prodded Larry. "You mean — about him bein' the first scribbler into New Chance?"

"No, the other thing," said Jennings. "He was a passenger in a stagecoach held up by the Reese gang."

9

The Valentine Touch

LARRY'S reaction was slow and controlled. He digested the reporter's words along with a well-chewed mouthful of ham. And his sun-browned face was impassive, his demeanor casual, when he drawled a rejoinder.

"Yeah, it likely did happen the way Russ told it. No reason a Denver reporter couldn't be a stage passenger."

"Must've been quite an experience," mused Jennings. "He claimed one of those hold-up artists took a shot at him. The bullet missed him, but the passenger beside him wasn't so fortunate."

"Ambushers," scowled Stretch. "Trigger-happy buzzards."

"I got to admit I was curious," said

213

Jennings. "I remember I said 'Now, Newcombe, why would any bandit want to shoot a harmless little feller like you?' And he just grinned back at me and . . . "

"He give you an answer?" prodded Larry.

"Oh, sure," nodded Jennings. "They had their faces covered with scarves and this one jasper, his scarf came untied. He saw Newcombe staring at him, and that's when he fired."

"Well, that's somethin' to brag about," shrugged Larry.

"Listen, getting back to you two — and your reputation . . . " began Jennings.

"Billy Reese is the big story hereabouts, you said," Stretch sternly remained him.

"No, I mean off the record, just between you and me." Jennings raised a hand. "My solemn oath as a journalist and a gentleman. This isn't for publication."

"Well?" frowned Larry.

214

"How much is true and how much is phoney baloney?" demanded Jennings. "I mean all the hashed-up stories I've read, all the outlaws you've fought, and the Indians . . ."

"We're just a couple fiddle-foots, peaceable and law-abidin'," declared Stretch.

"If it was up to us, we'd never fight at all," drawled Larry.

"We never yet started a hassle," Stretch earnestly assured the Chicago man. "Somebody else always starts it — and we kinda get mixed in."

"All right, if that's the way you want it," grinned Jennings. "Play it down. No bragging, and heavy on the modesty. But there are some exploits you can't deny, because they're on record with the Federal authorities. The near-revolution in Mexico. The kidnapping of Governor Brill's daughter. The attempted assassination of Crown Prince Rudolph."

"We've been a few places — done a few things," shrugged Larry.

"I want to thank you," chuckled Jennings, "for answering my direct question with such courteous ambiguity."

"We did what?" blinked Stretch.

"Let it pass." Jennings finished his coffee and got to his feet. "I'll see you later."

As the reporter moved away, the Texans rolled their first cigarettes and traded thoughtful glances.

"Now what?" asked Stretch.

"I'm wonderin' if we could find old newspapers at the Gazette office," muttered Larry.

"Well, sure you could," opined Stretch.

"I mean old copies of the Denver Clarion," said Larry. "If little Russ could identify one of Reese's old buddies — and if he saw that jasper right here in New Chance . . . ."

"Holy Hannah!" breathed Stretch.

"What I call a safe hunch," said Larry. "The killer spotted him and remembered him."

"And that's why Russ came up

dead." Stretch nodded vehemently. "Well, damnitall, runt, the whole outfit's likely hangin' around, likely plannin' on bustin' Reese out of the calaboose."

"Uh huh," grunted Larry. "And you can bet Russ wrote a story about the stagecoach raid. No newspaperman'd pass up such a chance."

"You're hopin' he described the galoot that lost his bandana," guessed Stretch.

"He just might have," nodded Larry. "Maybe the Denver papers don't travel this far south, but I want to be sure about that. So we'll go ask Doc."

They lit their cigarettes and, trading nods with the visiting journalists, quit the dining room. Moving through the lobby and out into Main Street, they donned their Stetsons and paused a moment. Larry's attention focussed on familiar figures, all members of the town council.

"Somethin's up," he observed.

Arnold Shell had quit the hotel a

few moments before, and now Oley Craydon was hurrying uptown from the stage depot. Cyrus Hindmarsh and Roscoe Lippert were coming out of the Eureka, waving to Shell and heading for the Gazette office, as was Milo Tweedy, just now emerged from the emporium.

"Somethin' fazin' 'em?" prodded Stretch.

"That'd be my guess," said Larry. "It looks like a special parley — some kind of emergency."

"You wouldn't want to butt in on 'em," Stretch supposed. "I mean, just to ask Doc about an old Denver paper."

"Butt in? Hell, no." Larry grinned mirthlessly. "That wouldn't be polite, would it now? But I've just figured a way to light a fire under the sonofabitch that killed little Russ."

"Flush him out, huh?"

"Damn right. Rig a trap. Force him into the open for a showdown."

"Sounds fine. But how?"

218

"Oh, with a little co-operation," drawled Larry, "from Mayor Tweedy and his pals."

"Think you an talk 'em into it?" asked Stretch.

"If that galoot in the jailhouse ain't Billy Reese, I've got 'em over a barrel," muttered Larry.

"And you don't think he *is* Billy?" challenged Stretch.

"Let's just say I'm a mite dubious," shrugged Larry.

"Where we headed?" demanded the taller Texan, as they moved off.

"Around back of the Gazette office," said Larry. "Might be Doc left a door unlocked, or a window. I got a sudden hankerin' to attend a meetin' — without an invite."

"You mean we're gonna snoop? Spy on 'em? Hell, runt, that's sneaky."

"Sure is. And I'm plumb ashamed."

"You don't sound like you're ashamed. Don't look ashamed neither."

Stretch was still uneasy when they reached the back alley. He glanced east and west while Larry tried the rear door, noting the alley was not exactly deserted. But the driver of the buck-board rolling past that rear door spared them only a casual glance, and the few pedestrians in sight were moving away from them, not looking backward.

"It's unlocked," Larry calmly announced. "Tag me."

They moved into a kitchen cluttered with stacks of cut newsprint, old type-boxes, ink containers and bundles of papers, early unsold editions of the Gazette. Stretch closed the door and followed his partner across to the curtained alcove leading to the newspaper office. Pausing there, they easily eavesdropped on New Chance's leading citizens.

It was more a debate than a discussion, more a heated wrangle than a debate, what with Tweedy talking non-stop and Lippert and the marshal clamoring to get a word in edgeways.

"More special guards . . . ?" Tweedy was heatedly protesting. "Hell's bells! I'm treasurer as well as mayor, and I'm tellin' you we're strainin' our budget!"

"Straining our budget be damned," scoffed the saloon-owner. "Our profits are rising every day. We can easily afford two extra guards."

"All you've given me is two," Cyrus pointed out. "And they can't squat on that front porch twenty-four hours a day. They got to sleep *sometime*."

"A homicidal lunatic running loose," complained Shell. "Two murders already — my guests scared stiff — and you penny-pinchers belly aching about a few extra dollars for a few extra deputies."

"Seems to me the whole deal's gettin' out of hand," fretted Craydon.

"Funny," said Doc, and he didn't sound amused. "That's exactly what *I* was about to say. Was it really such a great idea — passing that no-account off as the real Billy Reese?"

"Now, Doc, we all voted on it," chided Tweedy.

"For the sake of luring big city newspapermen to our town," agreed Doc. "But we should have thought about the kind of riff-raff, misfits and trouble-makers who'll travel a hundred miles for a sensational trial, a public hanging."

"Well, it ain't as if we're really gonna hang Appleyard," mumbled Cyrus.

"Which reminds me," said Doc. "The trial is less than two weeks away, and we still haven't planned Appleyard's escape."

"If anybody's got any suggestions . . . " began Tweedy.

"It would have to be handled carefully," warned Lippert. "In a way, we're beholden to him, so we have to be sure nobody takes a shot at him."

"I'm preparing another special edition," announced Doc. "It'll be a sell-out just like all the other special editions, and I should be happy. But I'm not. Our crazy scheme is *too* crazy."

"We're doin' fine," insisted Tweedy.

"Fooled everybody, didn't we? Even fooled those smart-aleck reporters from back east and . . ."

He stopped talking abruptly. His complexion changed to purple and his eyes dilated, while his cohorts loosed startled oaths. Larry had thrust the curtain aside and was ambling into he office with Stretch in tow, and now Doc Bayes was shrugging resignedly, looking a little older as he fumbled for pipe and tobacco pouch. Lippert glowered at the Texans. Shell and Craydon traded shocked glances and Cyrus froze where he stood, looking as guilty as a chicken-thief caught in the act.

"You fooled everybody," Larry assured the mayor, as he perched on the edge of Doc's desk.

"Except us," Stretch said smugly. Lippert had lurched to his feet, and now Stretch nudged him aside and helped himself to the vacated chair. Crossing his long legs, he blew a smoke-ring and bragged, "Takes us a while to catch on, but you know how it is, gents. Sooner or later . . . "

"You were spyin' on us!" accused Tweedy.

"Yup," nodded Stretch.

"He admits it!" raged Tweedy.

"Why not?" challenged Larry. "What're you gonna do? Sue us?"

"How much did you hear?" demanded Shell.

"I'll put it this way," drawled Larry. "It didn't set right with me — a cold-blooded killer like Reese wantin' to shoot himself, and just on account of some female that ran out on him. But I couldn't prove you jaspers were usin' a dead ringer — until just now."

"Well, hold on now . . . " began Craydon.

"Forget it, Oley," chided Doc, lighting his pipe. "Why waste time trying to brazen it out? They *know*. It's that simple."

"And now they're gonna blackmail us!" gasped Tweedy. "We'll have to pay 'em to keep our secret!"

"Tweedy, if you were some younger and a mite healthier," Larry grimly declared, "I'd bust your jaw for sayin' that."

"You mean you ain't gonna blackmail us?" Cyrus asked hopefully.

"Sure, I'm gonna blackmail you," said Larry. "But not for money."

"You've got your nerve," scowled Lippert.

"What I've got is the New Chance council," retorted Larry. He held out his hand palm-up. "Right here, savvy? I'm givin' the orders from here on, but I don't care a damn about that lame-brain in your jail — or the real Billy Reese. All I care about is a Texas scribbler who drowned in a horse trough. I want the skunk that killed him, and you fine citizens are gonna help set a trap for him."

"I'm not about to talk terms with a . . . " began Tweedy.

"Milo," said Doc.

"What?" frowned Tweedy.

"Shut up and listen," said Doc.

225

"What choice do we have?" sighed Shell.

"*No* choice," growled Larry. "You go along with my plan — or you end up lookin' mighty foolish. Those big city reporters . . . "

"Oh, hell!" groaned Craydon. "When they get through with us — New Chance'll be nothin' but a bad joke!"

"So we listen," Doc said firmly. "And, if Larry's scheme seems a little far-fetched, who are we to criticize? We — the leaders of this community — have conspired and deceived, lied and cheated, taken unfair advantage of a no-account who strongly resembles a famous outlaw, a fool, a would-be suicide." He heaved a sigh, mopped at his brow and told Larry, "Go ahead. There'll be no more interruptions."

Larry stubbed out his cigarette and talked for almost a quarter-hour, explaining his plan in simple terms, emphasizing the need for perfect timing and unstinting co-operation by all parties concerned — including the all-important Ed Appleyard.

When he had finished, his audience maintained their pensive silence for almost another 60 seconds. Cyrus voiced the first comment.

"The newspaper fellers gonna smell a rat."

"Or they might want to travel along with the wagon," warned Shell. "Reese was their reason for coming to New Chance, and they won't want to let him out of their sight."

"Nobody travels along with the wagon," said Larry. "Jake Sharney will be driver and, like I said, Doc'll stay in back with his patient."

"It won't look right," argued Cyrus. "My prisoner bein' moved to Brewer City with no lawman to ride guard on him."

"You're the only regular badge-toter in New Chance," Larry reminded him. "And there's a killer on the loose, don't forget. As for the prisoner, he's in no shape to make a break for it."

"I'll play my part," muttered Doc. "I

don't relish the prospect of an ambush — a gunfight — but I'll play my part. This is my penance, the price I have to pay for having collaborated in Milo's wild scheme."

"I agree with Arnie," frowned Lippert. "If those reporters follow the wagon, they could foul up your whole strategy."

"The marshal's gonna keep 'em busy," Larry said calmly. Nodding to Cyrus, he explained, "That'll be your special chore. Handle it right, and you'll hold 'em for an hour or more. In your office, or in the lobby of the hotel. Just so long as you keep 'em bunched."

"But how?" demanded Cyrus.

"You got the authority," declared Larry. "Two unsolved murders here — and you're still investigatin'. You've checked on every citizen and most of the visitors — and now you're gonna check on the scribblers. Why couldn't it be another newspaperman that killed little Russ and that Dean hombre?"

"They won't much appreciate that,"

mumbled Tweedy.

"Even so, it's a bona fide excuse for detaining them," said Doc. "They'll have to admit the logic of it. Be firm, Cyrus. Exert your authority — and hope for the best."

"If Valentine's plan works — and I'll agree it could succeed — those reporters will turn on us like hungry wolves," Shell gloomily predicted. "The jig will be up, my friends. The fat in the fire. We'll be shown up for what we are — seven impulsive jackasses. We dreamed up a crazy confidence trick, and were found out."

"Yes." Doc nodded dolefully. "When it's all over . . ."

"Follow my orders," advised Larry. "Do everything my way, and maybe it won't look so bad for you at the end."

"Some hopes," growled Lippert.

"Our goose'll be cooked," sighed Craydon.

"Jennings and his pards swallowed your lies," Larry pointed out. "Why

229

couldn't they swallow another lie?"

"What lie?" asked Shell.

"For instance?" prodded Stretch.

"Well like, for instance," shrugged Larry, "the whole idea behind your plan was to decoy Reese's old gang to New Chance."

"Hey now!" breathed Craydon.

"You arrested Reese's dead ringer," said Larry. "And you figured, if you spread the word you'd captured Reese himself, his old buddies'd come to New Chance to organize a jailbreak. Or maybe the real Reese would show up — to satisfy his curiosity."

"You know," Lippert said slowly, "that's not such a wild notion. The reporters might buy it!"

"Why, sure!" grinned Craydon. "And what do they care if it's all lies — just so long as it's a good story?"

"Today would be a bad time for setting your trap," Doc warned Larry. "There'll be a westbound stage passing through. Also we have two funerals this afternoon."

"Tomorrow — early," said Larry. "You'll start spreadin' the word right after sun-up, which gives you plenty time to explain it all to this Appleyard hombre. The rest'll be up to Doc — and Stretch and me."

"And Sharney?" demanded Craydon.

"Leave Jake to us," said Larry.

"Listen — uh — about that feller in the calaboose . . . " began Stretch.

"His chore is easy enough," shrugged Larry. "All he has to do is look miserable and keep his mouth shut."

"The wagon will be your responsibility, Oley," said Shell.

"No problem," said Craydon. "It'll be in the yard alongside the relay corral by midnight."

"Any more questions?" asked Larry.

"No more questions," Lippert said soberly. "The only thing left to say is — we don't deserve such a break."

"Amen to that," said Doc.

★ ★ ★

By mutual agreement, Molly Lamont and her admirer had decided to postpone their picnic. They would have returned to the township mid-afternoon when most of the population gathered in the New Chance cemetery to pay their last respects to couple of murder victims; a double funeral just didn't seem an appropriate conclusion to picnic.

Weems and his cronies stayed away. But Billy Reese was there, joining the crowd of inquisitive transients and deriving his own peculiar kind of pleasure from the experience.

There being no relatives to whom they could offer sympathy, Sam Jennings and his colleagues lined up to shake hands with the Texans and to assure them the little Denver journalist would be accorded a respectful obituary in the papers they represented.

By late afternoon, the town was bustling again, the reporters dictating messages at the telegraph office or writing follow-up stories on the two murders — liberally spiked with highly-imaginative comments which they attributed to such unlikely sources as Mayor Tweedy and the tongue tied Cyrus Hindmarsh; this time McWhirter managed to spell the names correctly.

Anticipating the next day's activity would prove strenuous, the Texans retired at 8.30 that night. They were wide awake and on the move again at 3.30 of the following morning, quitting the hotel quietly and making their way to the covered wagon waiting beside the corral near the stage depot.

A few minutes before sunrise, Cyrus stumbled out onto his office porch to rouse his volunteer guards.

"Fetch Doc!" he ordered at the top of his voice. "And you better get word to the mayor. Reese tried to kill himself!"

"Hell, Marshal! How in blazes . . . ?"

"Said he was hungry! I fixed his breakfast — and he tore his belly with a fork . . . !"

Like wildfire the news traveled about

233

the township and beyond. The shanty area was as empty as the saloons, hotels and rooming houses, the area fronting the jailhouse jampacked with excited locals and visitors for 20 minutes after Doc Bayes dashed into the building. From the porch, Tweedy harangued the surging throng and did his best to placate the impatient reporters.

"You'll get all the facts, sure, but how can I tell you if Billy's gonna live or die? Doc's with him now. When he's through, you'll get his statement."

"What I want to know is how did Reese get a knife?" yelled Freebold.

"No use blamin' the marshal," pleaded Tweedy. "Billy was quiet and peaceable, see? Claimed he was hungry, so Cyrus fixed him a dish of beans. And it wasn't a knife. Billy stabbed himself with the fork. You never saw the day a hot-shot lawman like Cyrus would give a prisoner a knife."

"He should've fed Billy through the bars," scowled Jennings. "With a spoon."

Wedged in the centre of the milling crowd, the unkempt stranger with the shoulder-length mane and long black beard spotted two of his old followers and chuckled to himself.

"They got plenty extra to fret about now. What happened to old Harp was a bad shock, but this is worse. Still hungry for the loot they are — and fearin' I'll die without talkin'."

The situation appealed to Billy Reese's twisted sense of humor. He revelled in it, while maintaining a placid exterior. To add to his amusement, Nate Rocklin glanced at him from less than 15 yards away and failed to recognize him.

Shoulder to shoulder with Weems, Rocklin muttered resentfully.

"Damn him, Silky! If he cashes in . . . !"

"You choose a helluva time and place to talk about it," Weems sourly chided. "Save your comments, damn you. Wait till we're far clear of this crowd."

Doc finally emerged from the law office with Cyrus. At once, the newspapermen pressed closer to the porch, bellowing a confusion of questions. Tweedy raised his hands in a plea for silence.

"Everybody quiet down! We're all anxious to hear what Doc says — so let him say it, for pity's sakes!"

Hefting his little valise, the medico advanced to the edge of the porch to address the throng.

"Severe abdominal injuries — self-inflicted," he announced. "There's a good chance Billy will recover to stand trial, but he'll need special treatment, and I just don't have the facilities for such intricate surgery. Only one thing we can do, and it *will* be done, I assure you. I'm taking him to Brewer City, west of the mountains. Some of you probably know they have a fully-equipped hospital at Brewer. Well, that's the place for Reese. Our only chance and — the sooner I get started . . . "

"How far to Brewer City?" demanded McWhirter.

"Is your patient fit to travel?" asked Harmon. "Can you be sure he'll survive the journey?"

"I'll be right beside him every mile of the way," declared Doc. "Yes, he could travel fairly comfortably. If my friend Oley Craydon will co-operate . . . "

"Anything, Doc," said the depot manager. "Just ask."

"Since we have no ambulance, we'll have to improvise," said Doc. "A wagon would be best, because Reese will have to travel prone. You could pad the wagonbed with blankets, make sure the stretcher is protected. All I need is a driver who knows the route."

"That's been arranged, Doc," nodded Cyrus. "We have a volunteer, a mighty reliable man."

"Just a minute!" called Freebold. "Is it your intention to take Billy to the Brewer City hospital all by yourself? Just you, the driver and the prisoner?"

237

"Reese is the most dangerous, the most treacherous resourceful . . . " began Harmon.

"Reese is incapable of movement," Doc said bluntly. "Confound it, I just got through treating him, so wouldn't *I* know? He's weak from extensive bleeding. Too weak to sit up, let alone stand or walk."

"I'll remind you gents that Marshal Hindmarsh is a town lawman," Tweedy said pompously. "He's responsible for keepin' the peace within the confines of New Chance Pass. And there's no call for an escort anyway. You heard what Doc said, Reese is helpless."

"How soon could you have the wagon ready?" Doc asked Craydon.

"Ten minutes," offered Craydon. "Fifteen at most."

"Right. I'll wait," said Doc. "Get a hustle on now."

"We'll be right behind you, Doc," announced Jennings.

"We'll all be following you," said McWhirter. "Hey, Joe, we'll rent a

238

buggy — any kind of rig — and . . . "

"The hotel will hold our baggage," opined Freebold. "We could all chip in, hire as many vehicles as we need."

"Just as long as there's room for my camera," insisted Kress.

"You won't be headin' for Brewer rightaway — and that's official," growled Cyrus. "Soon as the ambulance wagon leaves, I want you reporters assembled in the hotel lobby. And I mean *all* of you. That clear?"

★ ★ ★

"Now see here, Marshal . . . !" blustered Harmon.

"I got two murders on my hands and I'm still investigatin'," declared Cyrus. "And I ain't through interrogatin', see?"

"Interrogating?" cried Jennings. "For the love of Mike, are you gonna treat *us* as murder suspects?"

"I'm sure the marshal means no offense, gents," said Tweedy. "But he

239

has his duty, and you got to understand. Everybody had to be questioned. Even me. And the only parties he hasn't gotten around to are you and your colleagues. It's just routine, but it has to be done."

"Well, I'll be . . . !" began Freebold.

"There's some point to what he says," decided Harmon. "And besides, it'll be good for a few paragraphs."

"Oh, sure," nodded Bennett. "Human interest stuff. How a reporter feels — under interrogation by a genuine Western lawman."

When Jake Sharney drove the wagon out of the side alley, the special deputies used their muscle and the butts of their shotguns to force a path for the vehicle. He stalled the team just below the law office steps and, as Cyrus and Craydon began carrying the laden stretcher out, interested parties surged forward to study Appleyard's contorted face.

Well to the fore was Nate Rocklin.

10

Bait for the Noose

FIRST to retreat, struggling to reach the west fringe of that excited crowd, were Rocklin and Weems.

"Got a quick look at him, and that was enough," declared Rocklin, as they hurried toward the clutter of tents beyond the township.

"If you're sure . . ." began Weems.

"It's him all right," grinned Rocklin. "Hurt bad — but alive."

"Our last chance," frowned Weems. "And, by Judas, we can't afford to bungle it."

"How can we miss?" chuckled Rocklin. "All five of us. Only the wagon-driver and the sawbones between us and Billy!"

Also in retreat was the real Billy

Reese, hurrying back to his camp to saddle his horse and ready his rifle. This, he assured himself, was the ideal opportunity. Now at last he would wreak vengeance on the men who had fought so hard to destroy him.

"Had me trapped. Like a caged coyote I was, and all of 'em hollerin' like wolves. Thought I'd run out to be shot down when they started the shack burnin'. Never counted on me findin' that tunnel. All right, Silky, Nate, Karl and George — and little yeller-belly Dace. Now it's *my* turn!"

The stretcher-bearers were impeded in the act of lifting the prisoner into the wagonbed. Barring their way, the reporters insisted the blankets be lowered to reveal the wound. Kress set up his camera and, with a shrug of resignation, Cyrus uncovered Appleyard's torso — naked except for the criss-cross of plaster and bandage rising to his navel.

"By golly . . . !" gasped Freebold.

"Satisfied?" Doc asked harshly. "Or

do you wish me to uncover the wound — exposing him to infection?"

"I got a great picture, Leo!" yelled Kress. "Why'd you do it, Billy?" demanded Jennings.

"No questions," growled Doc. "Can't you see he's too weak to talk?" He gestured impatiently as he clambered into the wagon. "Raise him now, boys. Careful! Easy does it . . . !"

The patient, stretcher and all, was lifted into the wagonbed, deposited on a thick rug dead centre, cushioned at either side by mounds of sacks and blankets packed clear to the duckboards. The tailgate was raised and fitted into position, after which Cyrus and Craydon dropped to the ground and signaled the driver. When they caught their final glimpse of him, Doc Bayes was squatting by the stretcher and checking his patient's pulse.

Jake Sharney flicked the team with his reins and started the wagon rolling; the gapers impeding his progress had no option but to scurry clear.

The lawman-turned-barkeep remained silent until they had left the shanty town far behind and were approaching the western outlet of the pass. Right-handed, he delved under his jacket to caress the butt of the pistol rammed into his pants-belt.

"Like old times," he remarked.

"You're glad to be back in harness?" prodded Doc. "Not sore at Larry for talking you into it?"

"Sore?" grinned Jake. "I'm thankin' him."

"You already thanked me," Larry reminded him. Sprawled left of the stretcher, he thrust the blankets away, sat up and gulped air. On the right side, his partner followed his example. "Anyway, *I* ought to be thankin' *you*, Jake."

"Satisfy my curiosity," begged Doc. "Why Jake? Almost any citizen of New Chance would have volunteered."

"On Jake we can rely," drawled Larry.

"On account of," explained Stretch,

"this won't be his first run-in with a bunch of gunhawks."

"Special chore, Doc," said Larry. "You heeled and ready, Jake?"

"Heeled and ready," nodded Jake.

"Jake's in a vulnerable position, up front there," fretted the medico. "If they fire without warning . . ."

"I'm bettin' they'll block the trail, make it a regular hold-up," said Larry. "They want Reese alive."

"You're depending on the old rumors," protested Doc.

"I'm willin' to stake my life on the old rumors," growled Jake. "Reese had a pile of loot stashed someplace. Double-crossed his gang. They want him dead, sure, but they'll figure on scarin' a few answers out of him before they finish him off."

"So they ain't about to shoot at the wagon," opined Stretch. "Well — not rightaway."

"Don't much matter if *I* stop a slug," remarked Appleyard, sitting up. "When I think of how Clarissa ran off with . . ."

245

"Be kind to me, Appleyard," scowled Doc. "Stop whining about your unfaithful sweetheart. It's more than I can stomach right now."

"That reminds me — my stomach itches like all get-out," complained Appleyard. "All that consarned plaster . . . "

"You all that set on dyin', mister?" prodded Stretch.

"Work with us, keep your mouth shut and you could end up a live hero," offered Larry. "She'd read about you in the newspapers."

"My pitcher and all?" asked Appleyard.

"For sure," declared Larry. "And then she'd know what kind of a man she ran out on. You'd like that, wouldn't you?"

"I'll think on it," decided Appleyard.

"On the down-trail now," Jake called to them. "The pass is about a quarter-mile to our rear. Slopes left and right of us. A lot of rock. A lot of cover."

"What's dead ahead?" demanded Larry.

"We're gettin' near the first bend

— and this could be the place for it," muttered Jake. "Better get set."

"Remember, Doc," warned Larry. "Soon as we slow down, you burrow under them blankets — muy pronto."

"As if I'm apt to forget," mumbled Doc.

"Look on the bright side, Doc," urged Stretch. "Think of the big story you can write."

"If I live that long," growled Doc.

At the grim business of stalking his prey, Billy Reese considered himself an expert. He had followed his old cohorts out of New Chance Pass, staying clear of the trail and a respectful distance behind and above them. And now, because they were staked out, he too was in position, his vantagepoint a square boulder on a shelf of the slope north of the bend. Crouched there with his rifle lined on the waiting horsemen, he chuckled in unholy anticipation. Sitting their mounts behind a brush-clump right of the bend they were shielded from view of the approaching wagon, but in clear view of him.

Jake, skilled at handling any kind of team, made it a slow turn, growling at the horses while aiming a derisive leer at the five riders emerging from the brush to bar his way, bandanas drawn up to their eyes.

He stalled the wagon and got in the first word.

"This some kind of joke? What d'you think I'm haulin' — bullion?"

"Shuddup!" snarled Rocklin, brandishing his Colt.

With a grimace of exasperation, Jake discarded his reins and folded his arms.

"Follow orders and stay healthy," advised Weems. "You and the doctor aren't worth a dime to us. We're only interested in the wagon — and Reese."

"I don't savvy . . . " began Jake.

"You don't have to," countered Weems. He nodded to Earl and Sturm. "Move around back. Get the doctor out of there."

"Now!" growled Larry.

He clambered over Doc and Appleyard toward the tailgate while Stretch threw up the rightside canvas and showed his hands — both gun-filled — and Jake completed his cross-arm draw, whipping his Colt from his pants and blasting at Rocklin. Weems and Grose, in shock but lethal, opened fire at deadly short range. Bullets tore through the canvas and, while Doc and his 'patient' hugged the floor of the wagonbed, Stretch cut loose.

Earl and Sturm fired in frantic haste as Larry's head and shoulders appeared above the tailgate. With his first shot, he rendered Earl hatless and sent him crashing to the dust, blood trickling from his bullet-torn scalp. Sturm wheeled his mount and was about to fire over his shoulder, Larry was drawing a bead on him when, to his astonishment, his target jerked convulsively and slid from his mount.

Rocklin was down, his left arm rendered useless by Jake's fast-triggered slug, and now the ex-lawman was off the driver's seat and in the wagonbed, crouched beside Stretch. Larry vaulted over the tailgate and moved to the vehicle's right side, bellowing a warning to Weems and Grose.

"Drop the hardware and raise your hands! You can't win!"

He swung his six-gun toward Rocklin, who had sprung to his feet. The burly hard case triggered fast at Stretch and Jake, his bullet whining between their heads as they returned fire. Gaping in horror, Grose saw him spin crazily and sprawl on his back, his broad chest bloody in two places.

"Last chance!" growled Larry, his Colt leveled at Weems' chest. "We're too close, mister!"

"And your sidekick looks plumb nervous," observed Stretch. "Try usin' that gun — and you're a sure loser."

Grose made a whimpering sound. His gun slid from his trembling hand. Weems cursed bitterly, uncocked his weapon, flung it to the ground and snarled an accusation at Larry.

"You and Reese — in cahoots! *He* set this up!"

"That's enough gab," frowned Larry. "Get down off your horses."

He wasn't completely in command of the situation. The manner of Sturm's death still perplexed him. Had the man stopped a wild bullet triggered by one of his accomplices? And then, as Weems began dismounting, he got his answer. Simultaneous with the distant bark of a rifle, Weems wailed in agony and toppled. The rifle barked again as he thudded to the ground and, flopping beside him, Grose cocked an ear to another sound.

"Holy Hannah!" breathed Stretch.

The laughter was strident and triumphant, a sound to chill the blood.

"That's *him*!" gasped Grose, lurching to his feet. "Oh hell! It's Billy — payin' us off!"

He cried out in fear and agony as the rifle barked again and again. A bullet had torn a furrow atop his right shoulder. The impact threw him face-down, but he could still move. In panic, he began crawling under the wagon, while Doc raised his voice in angry protest.

"Hey! That last one near hit me!"

"Up the slope, runt!" warned Stretch. "I see him now — on a shelf up there!"

"Throw me your rifle," ordered Larry.

Stretch tossed his Winchester out. As he dropped to reach for it, Larry heard the sniper's weapon again. The bullet struck the rim of the right rear wheel and ricocheted, whining. Had he moved a second slower . . ."

Grabbing the rifle, he whirled and made for the base of the slope, running zig-zag. The sniper laughed wildly and cut loose with a savage burst and, with the fast-triggered slugs kicking up dust to either side of him, Larry realized the harrowing truth. The rumors hadn't exaggerated; killing was

252

Reese's pleasure.

Jake Sharney followed Larry's progress until he made the base of the slope and began climbing. Then, alerted by the scuffling sounds below, he changed position, moving across to hunker behind the driver's seat. Grose climbed up and parted the flaps to stare into the unwavering muzzle of Jake's long-barreled Colt.

"You're under arrest," Jake announced with relish. "Glory hallelujah! First time I've said it in years. It feels so good I think I'll say it again."

"Go ahead," urged Stretch. "Maybe he didn't hear you the first time."

"You're under arrest," repeated Jake.

"I *did* hear you the first time," groaned Grose. "Let me in there. I don't care what happens to me — only you gotta protect me from Billy!" He clambered into the wagonbed. Appleyard sat up, grinning. For an anguished moment he gaped at the bogus Billy Reese. "No! You can't be him . . . !"

"He'll faint now," predicted Doc. And Grose promptly fainted.

Larry had ascended to a boulder barely big enough to shield him. He squatted awkwardly, readying the Winchester for action, while Reese bounced three more slugs off the rock. Plainly, the crazed killer wasn't short on ammunition.

"He's had time to reload," Larry reflected. "All right. Somebody owes me a new hat."

He tugged off his Stetson, set it atop the rock and edged his face around its right side to scan the ledge above. He caught a fleeting glimpse of Reese as he triggered again, but wasn't given time to return fire. The hat skittered away, its crown torn, and Reese yelled derisively.

"Too old a trick to fool Bloody Billy!"

The killer's rifle barked again. Larry took a chance while the bullet ricocheted, moving clear of his cover and assuming a half-kneeling position, his sights on the ledge. For a moment, all he could see was the jerky movement of Reese's rifle-barrel, indicating he was levering a fresh shell into the breech. And then Reese's head and shoulders appeared behind the leveled weapon; a small target, but Larry's best chance. He sighted quickly, squeezed trigger and, with the recoil, saw Reese stagger clear of the shielding rock. Howling in pain and frustration, bleeding from the left shoulder, the killer tried to steady himself. And, by then, Larry was ready for his second shot. He aimed low, off-balancing his adversary by creasing his right calf. Reese toppled off the ledge, losing his grip of his weapon, slithering, rolling.

Larry tried to check his hectic descent but failed. He saw Reese hurtle past out of reach of his out-thrust arm. A small boulder momentarily stalled him. His head struck it with jarring force, and then he was rolling again, unconscious.

Stretch dropped from the wagon,

holstering his matched .45's. He reached the sprawled figure just as Larry finished his descent and, together, they hauled him upright.

"Kinda wild-lookin', ain't he?" remarked the taller Texan, observing the matted black mane, the long thick beard. "Hell, how did that jasper know this was Reese? He don't look nothin' like Eddie."

"It was the way he laughed, I guess," shrugged Larry.

At his insistence, Doc made Reese his first patient. While Jake rustled up a fire. Stretch tied the three dead men onto their horses and placed Grose and Earl side by side, their backs to a wagon-wheel. Both had regained consciousness, Grose whimpering from the agony of his bullet-torn shoulder, Earl mopping at his bloodied head and mumbling incoherently.

A stiff shot of whiskey revived Reese after Doc had cleaned and bound his wounds. He would have struggled upright had Stretch not pressed a cocked Colt to his belly.

"My Bowie's sharp enough," he remarked to his partner. "And you'll likely find a razor in the dude's saddlebag."

With the razor, Stretch's Bowie knife and a scissors borrowed from Doc, Larry played barber. He used Ed Appleyard as his model, cropping Reese's mane, trimming his beard, then shaving him. When it was done, Jake and the medico traded wondering glances and the prisoners were temporarily oblivious to their pain. Earl stared incredulously. Grose flinched and mumbled a plea.

"Don't let him near me!"

"It says a lot for the Reese influence," muttered Doc. "He's disarmed and helpless — and still they fear him."

"That other jasper," sighed Earl, blinking at Appleyard. "He kin to Billy?"

"I don't think so," said Jake.

"Who — me? Hell, no." Appleyard shook his head. "No thieves nor killers in my family. Only one I ever wanted to kill was me."

"Who is that sonofabitch?" demanded Reese.

"You never saw him before?" challenged Larry.

"He looks a whole lot like you," said Stretch.

"*Nobody* looks like me," scowled Reese. "There's only one Billy Reese." venting his spleen on Grose and Earl, deriding them, and bragging no jail could hold him. It spilled out of him unchecked and the Texans made no move to silence him. The loot coveted by his old cohorts had gone up in smoke. There was nothing left except his urge for vengeance. "You'll be next!" he raged. "I took care of Harp and Silky and Karl — and I'll sure as hell finish the job!"

"You heard what he said!" gasped Grose. "Hell! You gotta protect us!"

"That'll depend," Larry said grimly. "So far, you've said nothin' we don't already know."

"Ask me anything!" offered Grose.

"About the little feller," frowned Larry. "The Denver man."

"Him that drowned in a trough," growled Stretch.

"You already settled for him," shrugged Earl.

"It was big Nate — and Silky put him up to it," mumbled Grose, gesturing to the death horses. "The reporter feller, he ran into Silky outside the livery stable and, rightaway, Silky remembered him . . . "

"And Newcombe remembered *him*," said Larry.

"That's how it was," nodded Grose. "Silky showed his face for a couple minutes after we hit a stagecoach . . . "

"Three — maybe three and a half years ago," said Earl.

"The reporter saw him clear — and remembered him," said Grose. "And Silky knew this feller could talk him onto a gallows, so Nate went after him and . . . " He grimaced and bowed his head. "Damnit, I don't want to hang. I'll make a statement. Anything you want to know — about all the people Billy killed . . . "

"Doc," said Larry. "Soon as you've patched these heroes, we'll head back to New Chance."

"There'll be quite a reception committee," Doc warned. "I can't imagine what kind of wild story you're cooking up, but it had better be good. Convincing those reporters won't be easy."

"They'll buy what I tell 'em," opined Larry. "But only what *I* tell 'em, savvy? If you and your friends crave one last chance to save your faces, you have to go along with everything I say." Staring hard at Appleyard, he added, "That goes for you too."

"Well — uh — what's in it for me?" Appleyard asked eagerly.

"Like I said before, you end up a live hero," grinned Larry. "Just stay tight-mouthed and agree with everything I say."

"Well," shrugged Appleyard, "I guess that's fair enough."

★ ★ ★

The press conference was held in the barroom of the Eureka some 15 minutes after Reese and the only survivors of his old gang were installed in separate cells of the town jail. With two extra guards on duty there, Cyrus Hindmarsh could afford to join the other civic leaders seated around Roscoe Lippert's private table near the bar. The reporters occupied the other tables, hanging on Larry's every word, taking notes, occasionally interjecting questions. The only absentee was Joe Kress, who had photographed the prisoners and was now setting up his camera for a shot of the workmen beginning construction of the new gallows in Bonanza Road. Hubert Quince sat alone, making a group sketch of Mayor Tweedy and his fellow councilmen; it would eventually appear in the Tribune above the caption: "New Chance's Town Council Their Hour Of Triumph."

Enjoying his share of the limelight, Ed Appleyard perched on a bench by the side wall and nursed a short beer. He had demanded a double shot of rye but, suspecting strong booze might loosen his tongue, Larry had instructed Jake Sharney to draw him a short beer. Just the one.

Jake squatted on a high stool behind the bar. Predictably, Larry delivered his address from his favorite position, an elbow propped on the bar, a bootheel hooked on the brass rail, a full glass in his hand and Stretch right beside him.

Doc, Cyrus, Tweedy and Company strove to maintain their poise while Larry calmly offered his 'true and comprehensive' account of the whole affair. It had all begun, he told the reporters, with the arrival of Mister Edward Appleyard a few weeks ago. Noting Appleyard's striking resemblance to the infamous Billy Reese, Mayor

Tweedy and the marshal had devised an audacious plan with the full agreement of Doc Bayes and Messrs Lippert, Shell, Craydon and Webb, also the willing collaboration of Larry and Stretch. Their original plan didn't involve Billy Reese, who hadn't been heard of in over 3 years and might have ceased to exist for all they knew. But Reese's accomplices had never been apprehended. Remembering the rumors of a double-cross, with Reese having made off with the gang's accumulated loot, the council persuaded Appleyard to pose as Reese.

"Marshal Hindmarsh figured," Larry explained, "if word got around that Reese was bein' held for trial here, why, his old buddies'd hear about it and head straight for New Chance."

"The whole gang? Would they take such a risk?" challenged Jennings.

"It was a gamble," shrugged Larry. "But, the way Mayor Tweedy saw it, a *safe* gamble. They'd be playin' for high stakes, don't forget. Reese horded their loot — and it added up to a fortune."

"So this Appleyard guy was a voluntary decoy?" frowned McWhirter.

"Listen, this is the wildest, the craziest . . . " began Freebold.

"Call it wild, but don't call it crazy," countered Larry. "It worked, didn't it?"

"But you didn't anticipate the real Billy Reese would show up," accused Harmon.

"True enough," agreed Larry. "That was a surprise."

"Let me get this straight," begged Freebold. "It was Reese killed that guy in the alley after the gallows caught fire . . . "

"One of his old buddies, name of Harper Jardine," nodded Larry.

"But Russ Newcombe, the little guy from Denver . . . ?"

"Killed by one Nathan Rocklin, another member of the gang. Because he'd recognized one of 'em. Russ wasn't foolin' when he talked of the stage hold-up and how he could identify a man who'd ridden with Reese."

Bennett threw in his ten cents' worth.

"Why change the plan? Why couldn't you sit tight, wait for the Reese gang to try raiding the jail?"

"Mayor Tweedy and the marshal didn't count on so many visitors," drawled Larry. "If the gang attacked in daylight — or even at night — there'd be one helluva shootout. We were ready for 'em, but Mayor Tweedy reminded us he had a responsibility, the safety of hundreds of neutrals — includin' you newspapermen. In that kind of action there's too much danger some towner or visitor would stop a wild bullet."

"Very considerate of the mayor," frowned Harmon. "My respects, sir, and, on behalf of my colleagues, my deep appreciation."

"Well . . ." Tweedy shrugged modestly. "A man in my position just — uh — has to do his best."

"So that was the idea behind

265

Appleyard's fake suicide attempt?" asked Jennings. "You and Emerson hidden in the wagon — Doc and Mister Sharney willing to risk their lives — all for the sake of drawing Reese's men into the open? Well, I have to say it, Valentine. I've listened to your explanation and, from where I'm sitting, it's the most far-fetched mess of conniving and scheming, the wildest damn story I've ever heard."

"Sam," frowned Quince, closing his sketch-book.

"What?" frowned Jennings.

"How can anybody prove otherwise?" Quince asked gently.

"That's what *I* was about to say," shrugged Freebold. "If we don't accept Valentine's story, what's our alternative? How do we *prove* he's lying?"

"And here's another good question," offered McWhirter. "*Why* would he lie? What can he win by bamboozling us?"

"Larry and Stretch aren't publicity-minded," Quince pointed out. "Where the press is concerned, they're never co-operative. Downright antagonistic, in fact."

"So . . . ?" Larry finished his drink and eyed the reporters coldly, jaw jutting, right fist bunched on the bar-top. "Who's gonna be the first to call me a liar?"

"I accept Mister Valentine's expla-nation — with thanks," said Harmon. "Should we look a gift horse in the mouth, gentlemen? We came here to cover the trial and execution of a notorious desperado — and found much more than we hoped for."

"Two murders — and a whole lot more," nodded Freebold. "You're right, Cleave. Never a dull moment in New Chance."

"Well . . . " said Tweedy, with a complacent grin. "It's that kind of town."

Epilogue

SAM JENNINGS and his colleagues stayed on to cover the trial of William Lowell Reese. The jury was out for less than 15 minutes before delivering the predicted guilty verdict. Circuit-Judge Harold Morris pronounced the death sentence and, five days later, the infamous desperado paid for the crimes of which he had been charged — and a great many others — on the New Chance gallows.

Hubert Quince paid frequent visits to New Chance over the three months following the hanging, to the consternation of editor Maurice L. Harvey of the Chicago Tribune. Impressed by his persistence, Molly Lamont accepted his proposal. They were married in New Chance's Baptist chapel and traveled to Chicago right after the ceremony. Some four years later, the press artist resigned from the Tribune staff and, under the sponsorship of a millionaire meat-packer, became one of America's best-known portrait painters, also the founder of the Quince Art Gallery on Stratton Boulevard.

New Chance enjoyed a brief period of notoriety in the year following the events triggered by Ed Appleyard's only genuine suicide attempt. The first wave of excitement then fizzled out and Mayor Tweedy and his cronies anticipated with dismay a decline to the status of ghost town.

But Providence is kind to small children, drunks and God-fearing folk who say their prayers, and sometimes to small town officials. A partial collapse of the long-abandoned main tunnel of the Cafferty Mine necessitated the planting of charges to seal the entire shaft, this being the only method of ensuring no fossicking passer-by would wander in there to be buried by another fall.

The blast, though expertly supervised,

started an avalanche on the south slope of the pass. Later, volunteers clearing rubble at that side of town discovered quartz-rock dislodged by the explosion — and New Chance's second boom was soon under way.

For an obvious reason, Messrs Valentine and Emerson were unaware of these stirring events. Within an hour of Judge Morris' pronouncing sentence on Billy Reese, they were gone from New Chance. Unconcerned as to how Grose and Earl would fare on their day in court, no longer interested in the town, its citizens or its future, they saddled up and rode west.

Maybe they would never find their Utopia, a territory unmarred by violence and intrigue. But they would continue to seek it, still claiming to be law-abiding and peaceable, still Texas-stubborn.

CALABOOSE EXPRESS
WHISKEY GULCH
THE ALIBI TRAIL
SIX GUILTY MEN
FORT DILLON
IN PURSUIT OF QUINCEY BUDD
HAMMER'S HORDE
TWO GENTLEMEN FROM TEXAS
HARRIGAN'S STAR
TURN THE KEY ON EMERSON
ROUGH ROUTE TO RODD COUNTY
SEVEN KILLERS EAST
DAKOTA DEATH-TRAP
GOLD, GUNS & THE GIRL
RUCKUS AT GILA WELLS
LEGEND OF COYOTE FORD
ONE HELL OF A SHOWDOWN
EMERSON'S HEX
SIX GUN WEDDING
THE GOLD MOVERS
WILD NIGHT IN WIDOW'S PEAK
THE TINHORN MURDER CASE
TERROR FOR SALE
HOSTAGE HUNTERS
WILD WIDOW OF WOLF CREEK
THE LAWMAN WORE BLACK

THE DUDE MUST DIE
WAIT FOR THE JUDGE
HOLD 'EM BACK!
WELLS FARGO DECOYS
WE RIDE FOR CIRCLE 6
THE CANNON MOUND GANG
5 BULLETS FOR JUDGE BLAKE
BEQUEST TO A TEXAN

TOP HAND
Wade Everett

The Broken T was big. But no ranch is big enough to let a man hide from himself.

GUN WOLVES OF LOBO BASIN
Lee Floren

The Feud was a blood debt. When Smoke Talbot found the outlaws who gunned down his folks he aimed to nail their hide to the barn door.

SHOTGUN SHARKEY
Marshall Grover

The westbound coach carrying the indomitable Larry and Stretch headed for a shooting showdown.

FIGHTING RAMROD
Charles N. Heckelmann

Most men would have cut their losses, but Frazer counted the bullets in his guns and said he'd soak the range in blood before he'd give up another inch of what was his.

LONE GUN
Eric Allen

Smoke Blackbird had been away too long. The Lequires had seized the Blackbird farm, forcing the Indians and settlers off, and no one seemed willing to fight! He had to fight alone.

THE THIRD RIDER
Barry Cord

Mel Rawlins wasn't going to let anything stand in his way. His father was murdered, his two brothers gone. Now Mel rode for vengeance.

ARIZONA DRIFTERS
W. C. Tuttle

When drifting Dutton and Lonnie Steelman decide to become partners they find that they have a common enemy in the formidable Thurston brothers.

TOMBSTONE
Matt Braun

Wells Fargo paid Luke Starbuck to outgun the silver-thieving stagecoach gang at Tombstone. Before long Luke can see the only thing bearing fruit in this eldorado will be the gallows tree.

HIGH BORDER RIDERS
Lee Floren

Buckshot McKee and Tortilla Joe cut the trail of a border tough who was running Mexican beef into Texas. They stopped the smuggler in his tracks.

BRETT RANDALL, GAMBLER
E. B. Mann

Larry Day had the choice of running away from the law or of assuming a dead man's place. No matter what he decided he was bound to end up dead.

THE GUNSHARP
William R. Cox

The Eggerleys weren't very smart. They trained their sights on Will Carney and Arizona's biggest blood bath began.

THE DEPUTY OF SAN RIANO
Lawrence A. Keating and
Al. P. Nelson

When a man fell dead from his horse, Ed Grant was spotted riding away from the scene. The deputy sheriff rode out after him and came up against everything from gunfire to dynamite.

FARGO: MASSACRE RIVER
John Benteen

The ambushers up ahead had now blocked the road. Fargo's convoy was a jumble, a perfect target for the insurgents' weapons!

SUNDANCE: DEATH IN THE LAVA
John Benteen

The Modoc's captured the wagon train and its cargo of gold. But now the halfbreed they called Sundance was going after it . . .

HARSH RECKONING
Phil Ketchum

Five years of keeping himself alive in a brutal prison had made Brand tough and careless about who he gunned down . . .

FARGO: PANAMA GOLD
John Benteen

With foreign money behind him, Buckner was going to destroy the Panama Canal before it could be completed. Fargo's job was to stop Buckner.

FARGO:
THE SHARPSHOOTERS
John Benteen

The Canfield clan, thirty strong were raising hell in Texas. Fargo was tough enough to hold his own against the whole clan.

PISTOL LAW
Paul Evan Lehman

Lance Jones came back to Mustang for just one thing — revenge! Revenge on the people who had him thrown in jail.

HELL RIDERS
Steve Mensing

Wade Walker's kid brother, Duane, was locked up in the Silver City jail facing a rope at dawn. Wade was a ruthless outlaw, but he was smart, and he had vowed to have his brother out of jail before morning!

DESERT OF THE DAMNED
Nelson Nye

The law was after him for the murder of a marshal — a murder he didn't commit. Breen was after him for revenge — and Breen wouldn't stop at anything . . . blackmail, a frameup . . . or murder.

DAY OF THE COMANCHEROS
Steven C. Lawrence

Their very name struck terror into men's hearts — the Comancheros, a savage army of cutthroats who swept across Texas, leaving behind a bloodstained trail of robbery and murder.

SUNDANCE: SILENT ENEMY
John Benteen

A lone crazed Cheyenne was on a personal war path. They needed to pit one man against one crazed Indian. That man was Sundance.

LASSITER
Jack Slade

Lassiter wasn't the kind of man to listen to reason. Cross him once and he'll hold a grudge for years to come — if he let you live that long.

LAST STAGE TO GOMORRAH
Barry Cord

Jeff Carter, tough ex-riverboat gambler, now had himself a horse ranch that kept him free from gunfights and card games. Until Sturvesant of Wells Fargo showed up.

McALLISTER ON THE COMANCHE CROSSING
Matt Chisholm

The Comanche, McAllister owes them a life — and the trail is soaked with the blood of the men who had tried to outrun them before.

QUICK-TRIGGER COUNTRY
Clem Colt

Turkey Red hooked up with Curly Bill Graham's outlaw crew. But wholesale murder was out of Turk's line, so when range war flared he bucked the whole border gang alone . . .

CAMPAIGNING
Jim Miller

Ambushed on the Santa Fe trail, Sean Callahan is saved by two Indian strangers. But there'll be more lead and arrows flying before the band join Kit Carson against the Comanches.